Native Son

Nambi E. Kelley

Adapted from the novel by Richard Wright

A SAMUEL FRENCH ACTING EDITION

FOUNDED 1830

SAMUELFRENCH.COM
SAMUELFRENCH-LONDON.CO.UK

FOR PRODUCTION ENQUIRIES

UNITED STATES AND CANADA
Info@SamuelFrench.com
1-866-598-8449

UNITED KINGDOM AND EUROPE
Plays@SamuelFrench-London.co.uk
020-7255-4302

Each title is subject to availability from Samuel French, depending upon country of performance. Please be aware that *NATIVE SON* may not be licensed by Samuel French in your territory. Professional and amateur producers should contact the nearest Samuel French office or licensing partner to verify availability.

MUSIC USE NOTE

Licensees are solely responsible for obtaining formal written permission from copyright owners to use copyrighted music in the performance of this play and are strongly cautioned to do so. If no such permission is obtained by the licensee, then the licensee must use only original music that the licensee owns and controls. Licensees are solely responsible and liable for all music clearances and shall indemnify the copyright owners of the play(s) and their licensing agent, Samuel French, against any costs, expenses, losses and liabilities arising from the use of music by licensees. Please contact the appropriate music licensing authority in your territory for the rights to any incidental music.

IMPORTANT BILLING AND CREDIT REQUIREMENTS

If you have obtained performance rights to this title, please refer to your licensing agreement for important billing and credit requirements.

NATIVE SON premiered in a co-production between American Blues Theater and Court Theatre in Chicago, IL on September 20 & 21, 2014 under the direction of Seret Scott. Scenic design was by Regina Garcia, with lights by Marc Stubblefield, costumes by Melissa Torchia, and sound by Joshua Horvath. The Production Dramaturg was Shepsu Aakhu. The cast was as follows:

BIGGER...Jerod Haynes

THE BLACK RAT.....................................Eric Lynch

MARY.. Nora Fiffer

JAN .... Jeff Blim

HANNAH.......................................Shanesia Davis

BUDDY .... Edgar Sanchez

BESSIE... Tracey Bonner

MRS. DALTON................................ Carmen Roman

MR. DALTON ....James Leaming

BRITTEN...Joe Dempsey

GUS.......................................Tosin Morohunfola

VERA.. Tracey Bonner

Original stage adaptation by Paul Green and Richard Wright and produced in arrangement with the Paul Green Foundation – www.paulgreen.org

CHARACTERS

BIGGER – African-American man of 20

THE BLACK RAT – Afican-American male 20s, the voice inside Bigger's head

MARY – Caucasian female, early 20s, edgy and simultaneously precious

JAN – (pronounced JAN as in January) Caucasian male, 30s, well-intentioned with an edge; also plays **STORE OWNER, POLICE #2**, and others

HANNAH – African-American female, early 40s, tough, broken, the edge of anger, plays a variety of roles

BUDDY – African-American male to play teens, soft, a follower, also plays **NEGRO CLERK, JACKSON**, and others

BESSIE – African-American female to play teens to mid 20s; alcoholic, also plays **VERA, LESLIE**, and others

MRS. DALTON – Caucasian female, late 40s to early 50s, blind and well-intentioned; also plays **AGENT** and others

BRITTEN – Caucasian male, 40s-50s, main investigator, thrives on mischief; also plays **NEWSREEL V.O., MOVIE V.O., POLICE #1**, and others

SETTING

A labyrinth of Chicago's Black Belt and surrounding areas as it appears inside Bigger's mind.

TIME

A split second inside Bigger's mind when he runs from his crime, remembers, imagines, two cold and snowy winter days in December 1939 and beyond.

AUTHOR'S NOTE

Scenes represent a unit of thought in Bigger's mind. Scene breaks indicate a shift in Bigger's thought. For optimum clarity and connection, scene breaks should be ignored and the action performed continuous without an intermission.

Nambi Kelley's rendition of the book Native Son*, by Richard Wright is probably the most multi-faceted version, amongst many attempts to capture the essence of a book which the Library of Congress has now classified as one of the 100 best American works. Nambi Kelley is wonderfully apt at "playing" with space, time and circumstance. We feel Richard Wright would be captivated by the creation of the Black Rat as Bigger's alter ego, and would have enjoyed seeing night after night of a full house at the Court Theater, still mesmerized by a 21st century Bigger Thomas. A 21ST CENTURY NATIVE SON AT THE COURT- NOT TO BE MISSED.*

Julia and Malcolm Wright,
The Richard Wright Estate, Jan. 2015

FEAR

A Biggerlogue

(Lights rise on **BIGGER THOMAS**, *alone.)*

(He stands naked, dripping wet, and shivering.)

(Unidentifiable onlookers onlook.)

(A voice in the dark speaks **BIGGER**'s *thoughts.)*

THE BLACK RAT. *We all got two minds. How we see them seeing us. How we see our own self. But how they see you take over on the inside. And when you look in the mirror – You only see what they tell you you is. A black rat sonofabitch.*

*(***BIGGER** *opens his mouth to speak.)*

(Blackout.)

Scene One
With Mary

(Flashback. 2AM The **DALTON**'s.*)*

*(***MARY**, *20, slender, white, and precious is drunk.)*

BIGGER. Miss Dalton, where is your room?

MARY. Aw, shucks! Here, gimme a lift, I'm wobbly… Help me, Bigger. I'm stuck.

(He does.)

You're very nice, Bigger.

BIGGER. I don't know.

MARY. My! But you say the funniest things!

BIGGER. Maybe.

(She leans her head on his shoulder.)

MARY. You don't mind, do you?

BIGGER. I don't mind.

MARY. You know, for three hours you haven't said yes or no.

(She laughs. She sways.)

I sure am drunk…

*(***BIGGER** *watches her, helpless. She sways toward him.)*

BIGGER. I'd better help you.

(He catches her. His fingers graze the soft swelling of her breasts.)

MARY. Ooh. That tickles. I didn't know I was sho drunk!

(She leans more heavily against him.)

BIGGER. Try to stand up. Come on.

> *(She pulls heavily on him.)*

Come on. You got to get to your room. Come on, wake up!

> *(She goes completely limp.)*

Where's your room? Where's your room?!

> *(She rolled her eyes towards the door.)*

Is this really your room? Suppose it's Mr. and Mrs. Dalton's room?

> *(She does not respond.)*

Goddamn.

> *(Carefully he turns the knob of the door. Waits. Nothing happens. He pushes the door in quietly. A standing mirror greets him with his reflection holding the limp, drunk, white girl.)*

Goddamn.

> *(He grimaces at the reflection.)*

Here. Wake up, now. Stand up. No, don't put your face in my shoulder. Miss Dalton, I'm going to have to tighten my arms around you. No, no, no, no. Take your. No. Move your. Face. Lips. Away from mine – please.

> *(Her face comes towards his. She kisses him. Instinctually, he kisses her back then pushes her away.)*

No. Stand up. Stand.

> *(He stands her on her feet.)*

Good.

> *(She sways again, falling.)*

Oh no, please. Don't fall, don't –

> *(He tightens his arms around her waist. She kisses him again.)*

Goddamn crazy woman.

(He kisses her back, lifts her and lays her on the bed.)

MARY. You're...very...nice, Bigger...

(He kisses her again and lays on top of her. She grinds him, hard.)

Very...nice...

*(The door suddenly creeks. **BIGGER** sits straight up. In the mirror reflected is a white blur by the door.)*

MRS. DALTON. Mary?

*(**BIGGER** turns to see **MRS. DALTON**, **MARY**'s blind mother. He holds his breath. **MARY** mumbles, almost inaudibly.)*

Mary?

*(**MARY** tries to rise. **BIGGER** quickly pushes her head back to her pillow.)*

Mary? Are you asleep?

*(**MARY** tries to rise again. **MRS. DALTON** walks towards the bed.)*

I hear you moving about –

*(**BIGGER** grabs a pillow and covers **MARY**'s face. **MARY** surges upward. He lays his whole body on top of the pillow. **MARY** sighs.)*

Mary!

*(**MARY**'s fingers loosen. Then, her body is still. **MRS. DALTON** now stands over the bed. She sniffs the air taking a quick step back.)*

You reek of liquor!

*(She kneels. Whispering. In prayer. Exits. Silence. **BIGGER** goes to **MARY**'s bed.)*

BIGGER. Miss Dalton?

*(His hand moves toward her, but stop mid-air. **MARY**'s mouth and eyes are open.)*

Miss Dalton... She's – she's she's –

> (**BIGGER** *starts to hyperventilate. He snatches his hand away, knocking into the standing mirror. The mirror cracks but does not break, like a windshield upon impact.* **BIGGER** *whirls around to see,* **THE BLACK RAT** *reflected in the cracked pieces of* **BIGGER**'s *reflection.*)

THE BLACK RAT. And when you look in the mirror
You only see what they tell you you is –

THE BLACK RAT.	**BIGGER**.
A black rat sonofabitch.	A black rat sonofabitch.

> (**THE BLACK RAT**, *a young Black man of 20, is the spit and image of* **BIGGER**. *He lights a cigarette. Unlike the manchildness of* **BIGGER**, *he is very much a man with an even harder edge.* **BIGGER** *[he] lock eyes [with himself].*)

BIGGER. Dead?

THE BLACK RAT. Dead.

BIGGER. And I killed her?

THE BLACK RAT. And I killed her. A rich white girl. I am a murderer. A Negro murderer. A Black murderer.

BIGGER.	**THE BLACK RAT**.
They will kill me.	They will kill me.

> (**BIGGER** *starts to hyperventilate.*)

THE BLACK RAT. This is how Bigger was Born.

> (*An alarm clock sounds.*)

> (*Lights.*)

Scene Two
The Black Rat is Born

(Lights. 9AM. The same day.)

*(***BIGGER***'s home.)*

*(The alarm clock continues as **BIGGER** chases a huge black rat with iron skillets gripped tightly in his hands. **THE BLACK RAT** is there.)*

BIGGER. Rat Sonofabitch! I'll kill you!

HANNAH. Not him again this early in the day!

VERA. He so black and ugly!

HANNAH. Vera! Buddy! Climb up on the bed!

BUDDY. Ain't scared of a stinkin' rat!

BIGGER. He could cut your throat!

BUDDY. Look at him, he smiling!

VERA. He a foot long –!

HANNAH. That's how they grow 'em where we live!

BIGGER. Dalton Realty Home of Kings.

VERA. Get him, Bigger!

BUDDY. He'll get 'em!

HANNAH. There he is again!

BUDDY. Throw the skillet!

HANNAH. Hit 'em!

*(***BIGGER*** throws his skillet at the ferocious rat.)*

BUDDY. Got 'em!

THE BLACK RAT. Ouch.

*(***BIGGER*** repeatedly pounds the rat's head.)*

BIGGER. *(as he pounds)* I'm the rat bastard, huh? You goddamn sonofabitch! Grinning at me! I see you –!

*(The **RAT** is clearly dead. Yet **BIGGER** keeps pounding.)*

VERA. Bigger!

HANNAH. Lord, Lord have mercy, son...stop it, stop it –!

BIGGER. But whose dead now, huh? Whose bleeding now? Huh? Huh? Sonofabitch.

> *(BIGGER stops, suddenly he looks at the RAT, seeing its blood and guts everywhere. They all stare at BIGGER. Incredulous at the extent of his rage.)*

HANNAH. Throw him in the trash and clean yourself up. Can't be dirty when you meet the Dalton's at 5:30 for that chauffeur job. Go on, son. That black rat is dead.

BIGGER. Dead?

> *(A flying plane outside the window catches BIGGER's eye.)*

> *(Lights.)*

Scene Three
With Buddy

(Lights.)

(Later.)

*(**BIGGER** still watches the plane.)*

*(They shoot pool. **THE BLACK RAT** shoots at a nearby table as he listens.)*

BIGGER. They so alive. White boys sure can fly.

> *(**BIGGER** juts out his arms like a child and "flies" around the room.)*

Control tower, requesting clearance for landing!

BUDDY. This is control tower. Land your fool ass down at that pool table. Over.

BIGGER. Goddamn you, Buddy. I could, you know. I could fly.

THE BLACK RAT. Yeah. If you wasn't black and if you had some money and if they'd let you go to that aviation school, you *could* fly a plane.

BUDDY. Too damn early in the day to dream.

BIGGER. Don't you want nothing? Solid, side pocket.

BUDDY. Your shoot.

BIGGER. Done settled enough fights 'tween our folks...you could learn to be a Negro judge! Striped, corner.

BUDDY. That's dumb.

BIGGER. Not dumb. You also got a knack for numbers, you could –

BUDDY. Run numbers.

BIGGER. Naw. Something better.

BUDDY. Something better? Yeah, right. Say, you going over to the Dalton's later for that chauffeur job?

THE BLACK RAT. I gonna be driving a Cadilac! Or a Dusseldorf!

BIGGER. Yeah, I guess.

BUDDY. "Yeah, I guess"? Now you really dumb!

BIGGER. Buddy –?!

BUDDY. What?

THE BLACK RAT. Easy…

BIGGER. Your shot.

BUDDY. You talk like you don't want that chauffeur job.

BIGGER. I want it, just seem like –

> (**BIGGER** *looks at the sky. Watches the plane vanish.*)

They own the world.

NEWSREEL. *(voice over)* They own the world –

> *(Lights.)*

Scene Four
With Buddy

(Later.)

(The Regal Theatre. **BIGGER** *and* **BUDDY**. *Movie goers and* **THE BLACK RAT** *nearby watch a* **NEWSREEL**.*)*

NEWSREEL. *(voice over) – The daughters of the rich. These debutantes represent over four billion dollars of America's wealth –*

(The voice over continues indiscernibly.)

BIGGER. Sure wish I had my Bessie with me now.

BUDDY. You take that chauffeur job you can get you a better girl than Bessie.

BIGGER. She better than what you ain't got.

THE BLACK RAT. She a drunk.

*(***BIGGER**, *closes his eyes, begins squeezing his manhood.)*

BUDDY. Why your eyes closed? You at it again?

BIGGER. Polishing my nightstick. They own everything. But I own something too.

BUDDY. I'll beat you!

BIGGER. The hell you won't, kid!

(The boys giggle as they "race." **BIGGER** *and* **BUDDY** *repeatedly squeeze their manhood, racing.* **BUDDY** *leans forward, stretches his legs rigidly.)*

BUDDY. Yee-eeah… I win!

*(***BIGGER** *leans forward, stretches his legs rigidly.)*

BIGGER. I'm…gone too. You pull off fast.

BUDDY. Cause that white girl on the newsreel is a hot-looking number –

BIGGER. What white girl?

(Lights.)

Scene Five
With Daltons

(Lights.)

(Later.)

*(**MARY**'s voice ringing throughout the house.)*

MARY. Oh, Father!

THE BLACK RAT. That white girl.

> *(**BIGGER** opens his eyes. He turns to see **MARY**. **DALTON** entering. **MRS**. **DALTON** interviews **BIGGER**. **THE BLACK RAT** is there.)*

MARY. Oh, is this the new chauffeur father has approved?

MRS. **DALTON**. Perhaps. I'm giving him a second interview now. What do you want, Mary?

MARY. Will Daddy get the tickets for Orchestra Hall?

MRS. **DALTON**. Yes, now run along –

MARY. *(to **BIGGER**)* Hello.

BIGGER. Good evening, mam.

> *(**MARY** moves gets right in **BIGGER**'s face.)*

MRS. **DALTON**. Mary, why are you so close to the boy?

MARY. Do you belong to a union?

MRS. **DALTON**. Mary!

MARY. Well, Mother, he should! Since he's working for us, maybe Bigger things will happen for him, something bigger. *(to **BIGGER**)* Do you?

THE BLACK RAT. She gonna make me lose this job.

MRS. **DALTON**. Leave him alone, Mary!

MARY. All right, Madame Capitalist!

> *(to **BIGGER**.)*

Isn't she a capitalist?

MRS. **DALTON**. Mary, please! He doesn't even know what a "capitalist" is. Forgive her, Bigger.

MARY. Bigger? What a name. Toot-a-loo, Mr. Bigger. Fuddy duddy Mommy. Kiss.

(**MARY** *blows her mother a kiss and exits.*)

MRS. DALTON. My daughter. I'm sure you've seen her on the newsreels running off with that Communist?

(*Lights.*)

NEWSREEL (*voice over*) *Papa Dalton denounces Jan Erlone, a known Communist.*

(*Lights.*)

BIGGER. A communist, no mam.

MRS. DALTON. Oh. Well. My husband and Relief said you live at 3721 South Indiana with your brother, sister, and mother?

(*Lights.*)

Scene Six
With Family

(Lights.)

(Earlier.)

*(**BIGGER** and **THE BLACK RAT** sit at the breakfast table with family.)*

HANNAH. You listening to your mother? Remember you have to see the Daltons at 5:30 for that chauffeur job –

BUDDY. Aw, lay off him!

HANNAH. You shut your mouth, Buddy!

BUDDY. Aw, Ma!

HANNAH. Bigger when your daddy was your age –

THE BLACK RAT. Here we go –

HANNAH. – He took three jobs to support us all –

BUDDY. And where Daddy now?

HANNAH. Buddy! Bigger, you are already twenty. When are you going to become a man?

BUDDY. He been a man!

HANNAH. That's it, Buddy. Go pick me a switch.

BUDDY. It's fifteen degrees outside!

HANNAH. It's Chicago. Go!

> *(**BUDDY** obeys.)*

Vera, honey, go practice your sewing.

VERA. You gonna talk to him 'bout throwin' that dead rat at me?

HANNAH. Girl!

> *(**VERA** sucks her teeth.)*

Don't suck your teeth at me, girl!

> *(**VERA** exits.)*

Bigger. You the most no-countest man I ever seen in all my life. Even when the relief offers you a job you won't take it till they threaten to cut off our food and starve us.

BIGGER. Aw for Chrissakes!

HANNAH. You don't like me saying it? You can get out. We can live in one room just like we living now, even with you gone. Go live with that no good gang of yours. Got to be a man now, son. Got to stop being upset about your father –!

> (**BIGGER** *turns his back on them, grabs and tucks his gun in his pants, only seen by* **THE BLACK RAT**.)
>
> (*Lights.*)

Scene Seven
With Daltons

(Lights.)

(Later.)

(DALTON. BIGGER. THE BLACK RAT.)

MRS. DALTON. My husband's father passed down the South Side Real Estate Company to him. And so, 3721, where you live, is our property.

THE BLACK RAT. Dalton Realty! Home of Kings!

BIGGER. Yessum.

MRS. DALTON. And we are supporters of the National Association for the Advancement of Colored People. Did you ever hear of that organization?

THE BLACK RAT. Negro leaders ain't worth – Don't say that.

BIGGER. No mam.

MRS. DALTON. Well… The relief people said like most black boys you were in reform school and always in trouble. My husband was a boy once, we think we can understand these things. He even was in such a place. Once. Well, not quite. A…boarding school.

BIGGER. Yessum.

MRS. DALTON. My naughy husband snuck off to an anti-lynching rally down in Bughouse Square. His father followed him and dragged him out of there so fast he was on the next train out of Union Station.

BIGGER. Yessum.

MRS. DALTON. His father never thought he'd give away his millions to every Negro organization he could find. Yes, that boarding school sure did shape him up. We are more alike than it seems, Bigger.

> *(**THE BLACK RAT** chuckles. **BIGGER** reacts to this internal thought.)*

Gesundheit.

BIGGER. Uh…thank you, mam.

MRS. DALTON. Now. Why did they send you to reform school?

BIGGER. They said I was stealing. But I wasn't.

MRS. DALTON. Are you sure? They say you can drive a car. But if you steal –

(Lights on **HANNAH**.*)*

HANNAH. The only stealing you should be doing is for the Lord, Bigger.

(She sings.)

STEAL AWAY/
STEAL AWAY/
STEAL AWAY TO JESUS…/

(Lights out on **HANNAH**.*)*

BIGGER. Oh, no mam, just like I told Mr. Dalton, I don't steal.

(Lights.)

Scene Eight
With Buddy

(Lights.)

(Earlier.)

BIGGER. Let's clean out Old Blums Deli later.

BUDDY. You planning mischief this early in the day?

THE BLACK RAT. What is he, an old lady?

BUDDY. And Blum keep a gun. Suppose he beat us to it?

BIGGER. You scared 'cause he a white man?

BUDDY. The hell I'm scared! And ain't you supposed to meet Dalton this afternoon?

BIGGER. We'll do it before then.

THE BLACK RAT.	**BIGGER.**
Between three and four ain't nobody in the store but the old man. One of us'll stay outside and keep watch –	Between three and four ain't nobody in the store but the old man. One of us'll stay outside and keep watch –

BIGGER. One of us'll go inside and throw a gun on old Blum –

BUDDY. I thought we said we wasn't never going to use a gun.

BIGGER. Look. Can't you see? This is something *big*. They can't see us doing something like that. But we can do it. Gus said he'd meet us too.

BUDDY. Gus coming?

BIGGER. If us niggers ain't scared.

(Silence.)

Goddammit! Say something!

(Buddy stands. Bigger tightens.)

BUDDY. I'm in.

BIGGER. Meet here at 3?

THE BLACK RAT. Buddy scared.

BUDDY. You scared I'm going to say yes.

BIGGER. Say that again and I'll sink that ball in your goddamn mouth!

THE BLACK RAT. Shhhhh, easy –

BUDDY. You scared you'll have to do the job!

*(**BIGGER** leaps at him.)*

(Lights.)

Scene Nine
With Family

*(**BIGGER** to his **MA** at the table.)*

(Earlier.)

BIGGER. Ma, I told you I'd take the goddamn job!

(Lights.)

Scene Ten
With Daltons

(Lights.)

(Later.)

MRS. DALTON. Good then. I'll have my husband give you the job.

BIGGER. Yessum.

MRS. DALTON. You'll also have to tend the furnace. Goodness! You must be parched. Follow me.

(They cross to the kitchen.)

*(***BIGGER*** turns to the kitchen to find a glass. Behind him,* **MRS. DALTON,** *holding* **THE WHITE CAT** *[a hand puppet manipulated by* **MRS. DALTON***], appears from nowhere, listening.* **BIGGER** *turns to see her, startled. He and* **THE BLACK RAT** *silently watch her.)*

MRS. DALTON. You must be thinking I know exactly where you're standing?

BIGGER. Yessum.

MRS. DALTON. I think you'll find a glass just to your right.

BIGGER. Yessum.

MRS. DALTON. It's true what they say about us blind. The other senses do become sharper. My frivolous youthful taunting during prohibition with some bad rot gut replaced my perfect eyes for perfect ears.

BIGGER. Mam?

MRS. DALTON. I was a naughty girl who drank even naughtier liquor and now my eyes are for naught.

BIGGER. Yessum.

MRS. DALTON. Oh! If I could see your face! I imagine you. Handsome. Tall. Black like night. Do you wear glasses, son?

BIGGER. No, Mam.

MRS. DALTON. Ah! Perfect vision?

BIGGER. I reckon, Mam.

MRS. DALTON. Just like a pilot.

BIGGER. Mam?

MRS. DALTON. Oh yes! To be able to fly, one must be able to see, boy.

  (Lights.)

Scene Eleven
With Buddy

(Lights.)

(Earlier.)

(BIGGER *and* **BUDDY.)**

BIGGER. Man, I could fly, but white folks don't let us do nothing!

BUDDY. You say that like you just finding that out. Hey, I heard *Trader Horn*'s on at the Regal.

BIGGER. Why don't White folks let us run ships and fly planes?

BUDDY. That movie about that white girl raised by Africans!

BIGGER. And why they make us live in one corner of the city?

BUDDY. A white girl raised by Africans!

BIGGER. I wish – wish – someday there would be a Black man who could whip Black people into a tight band and together we could…could –

BUDDY. Make a stand against *them?*

BIGGER. Yeah!

BUDDY. Yeah right. She even wears a loin cloth!

(BUDDY *laughs.)*

THE BLACK RAT. Aw, forget about him.

BIGGER. Goddamnit! Listen!

THE BLACK RAT. Quit thinkin' about it, you'll go nuts.

BUDDY. Bigger?! Picture it. Loin cloth!

BIGGER. You know where "they" live?

MRS. DALTON. *(offstage)* You're to live in the back room above the kitchen –

(BIGGER *doubles his fist and hits his stomach.)*

BIGGER. Right down here in my stomach. Like fire.

(Lights.)

Scene Twelve
With Daltons

(Lights.)

(Later.)

MRS. DALTON. Did you ever fire a furnace before, son?

BIGGER. No mam.

MRS. DALTON. My husband will show you. Ah, I love the roar of a fire. I hear everything. For instance, you've finished your glass, please, pour yourself another.

BIGGER. Thank you, Mam.

(He does.)

MRS. DALTON. How far did you go in school?

BIGGER. To the eighth grade, mam.

MRS. DALTON. I never finished school. Couldn't see myself going back there after how I lost my eyes. Now you've met my Mary…

BIGGER. Yessum.

MRS. DALTON. Her hair I've never seen. My husband assured me when she was maturing that her hair color was just like mine. Not that fire red like his side of the family. That means something. To see yourself reflected in another human being, even if it's only in your mind, is everything in life. Do you understand, son?

THE BLACK RAT. Why is that cat looking at me like that?

*(***THE WHITE CAT*** swats at ***THE BLACK RAT***.)*

Cat!

MRS. DALTON. No Whitey! Forgive him.

THE BLACK RAT. I'm watching you. Whitey.

*(***THE WHITE CAT*** eyes ***THE BLACK RAT***.)*

MRS. DALTON. Other than Whitey's mischief, nothing ever happens around here.

(Lights.)

Scene Thirteen
With Buddy

(Lights.)

(Earlier.)

(BIGGER, THE BLACK RAT, BUDDY, *and* **GUS**
shoot pool.)

BIGGER. Goddamnit, nothing ever happens around here!
…Let's play "white!"

BUDDY. Aw hell, not again.

(BIGGER *makes a "telephone" with his hand.)*

BIGGER. *(in his best white man imitation)* "This is Mr. J.P.
Morgan speaking."

BUDDY. Nigger you nuts.

BIGGER. Nigger I said, "This is Mr. J.P. Morgan speaking."

BUDDY. All right. I'll play. "Yessuh Mr. Morgan."

BIGGER. "I want you to sell twenty thousand shares of U.S.
Steel 'cause I have all the money in the world."

BUDDY. "Yessuh, Mr. Morgan!"

(BIGGER *picks up his "telephone" again.)*

BIGGER. "General!"

BUDDY. Lawd, today!

BIGGER. "This is the President of the United States
speaking!"

BUDDY. "Yessuh, Mr. President!"

BIGGER. "The niggers is raising sand all over the country.
Attack them! We've got to do something with these
black folks."

BUDDY. "Oh! If it's about the niggers, I'll be right there,
   Mr. President!"

BIGGER. "Left flank! March!"

>   (**BUDDY** *salutes and clicks his heels. Silence. Then
>   they burst into laughter.*)

BUDDY. Say, what's a "left flank?"

BIGGER. I don't know, heard it in the movies once. Man,
   White folks don't let us do nothing!

Scene Fourteen
With Daltons

(Lights.)

(Later.)

MRS. DALTON. It's nothing to learn the furnace. Our last boy learned to tend fire easily. Ours is a self-feeder. Your biggest trouble will be taking out the ashes and sweeping or it gets cold upstairs. Can you handle that?

BIGGER. Yessum.

MRS. DALTON. Good. And you'll do all the driving for us.

THE BLACK RAT. What kind of car they gonna give me? I hope it's a Packard or a Lincoln or a Rolls Royce!

MRS. DALTON. At 8:30 tonight, you will drive my daughter out to the University and wait for her. It's best if you refer to her as Miss –

(Lights.)

Scene Fifteen
With Buddy

(Lights.)

(Earlier.)

(The Regal Theater. **BIGGER** *and* **BUDDY** *have just finished "racing." Others and* **THE BLACK RAT** *are there. A* **NEWSREEL** *blares.)*

NEWSREEL. *(voice over)* – *Mary Dalton, daughter of Chicago's Henry Dalton, 4605 Drexel Boulevard –*

*(***BIGGER*** looks up. Wide shot of* **JAN** *chasing* **MARY.***)*

BIGGER. Say...that gal there kissing that man, that's the daughter of the guy I'm going to see about that job –

BUDDY. Shucks, I hear rich white girls'll go to bed with anything from a poodle on up. You get too much to handle, you let me know.

NEWSREEL. *(voice over) Papa Dalton denounces Jan Erlone, a known Communist.*

BIGGER. Communist? What's a communist?

(Lights.)

Scene Sixteen
With Daltons

(Lights.)

(Later.)

(MRS. DALTON *and* **BIGGER.)**

MRS. DALTON. I'm sure you've seen on the newsreels my daughter running off with that Communist?

(Lights.)

Scene Seventeen
With Buddy

(Lights.)

(Earlier.)

(BUDDY *and* **BIGGER.***)*

BUDDY. It's a race of people who live in Russia, ain't it?

BIGGER. Damn if I know.

BUDDY. That guy kissing that girl was a Communist and her folks didn't like it.

BIGGER. Rich folks must not like Communists.

(On screen, a horn blows.)

BUDDY. "Trader Horn" is on!

(Black men and women in loincloths whirling in wild African dances and beating drums fill the screen.)

MOVIE. *(voice over)* "*Trader Horn* presents savages on The Dark Continent."

BIGGER. Ma know you watch this stuff?

(To **BIGGER***'s eyes,* **MARY DALTON** *appears on screen in a loincloth alongside the black men and women.)*

THE BLACK RAT. Miss Dalton?

MOVIE. *(voice over)* "She's beautiful. Savage as any of the black ones, a She Devil, a Queen of the Jungle –"

BUDDY. Here's the best part –

MOVIE. *(voice over)* "…starring Edwina Booth as The White Goddess of Paganism in… *Trader Horn!*"

*(***MARY** *cracks a whip. The black men and women cower.* **MARY** *smiles, larger than life.)*

MARY. Work for me. Bigger things will happen. Something. Bigger.

BIGGER. Yeah. Something Bigger.

(**MARY** *winks at* **BIGGER**. *"Trader Horn" ends.*
BIGGER *is dreamy-eyed.*)

BUDDY. It's almost 3 o'clock. Come on.

BIGGER.	**MARY**.
Something big.	Something big.

BUDDY. Wake up, Bigger. My first "job" awaits. Blums! Gotta go meet Gus.

THE BLACK RAT. Not sure about this.

BIGGER. Let's go.

(*Lights.*)

Scene Eighteen
With Buddy

(Lights.)

(Earlier.)

(BUDDY *and* **BIGGER** *walk in. No* **GUS.)**

BUDDY. You shakin'.

BIGGER. That's what's called adrenaline, kid. If Gus make us miss this Blum job I'll fix 'im so help me.

BUDDY. Word is ain't nobody got more guts'n Gus.

BIGGER. Aw, shut your trap. Break 'em. For I tell Ma you here.

> **(BUDDY** *starts the pool game.)*

BUDDY. I'm 16. And a half.

THE BLACK RAT. You wet. Behind the ears.

BIGGER. Say, I betcha two bits you can't make it.

> **(BUDDY** *shoots a ball shot into a side pocket.)*

BUDDY. You would've lost.

> *(Still no* **GUS.)**

BIGGER. Bastard oughtn't be late.

BUDDY. I hear he always show up minutes before a job.

BIGGER. You sure hear a lot, kid.

BUDDY. Ain't no goddamn kid!

BIGGER. Gus late cause he nervous

BUDDY. ...Or maybe you are.

> *(Lights.)*

Scene Nineteen
With Mary

(Lights.)

(Later.)

*(**MARY** in car with **BIGGER**.)*

MARY. I make you nervous, Bigger?

THE BLACK RAT. Careful.

BIGGER. No mam.

MARY. I'm not going to the University. I want you to take me to the Loop. But you can forget I said that.

BIGGER. Mam?

MARY. I think I can trust you. After all, I'm on your side. You aren't a tattle tale are you?

BIGGER. No mam, not a tattle tale, mam.

MARY. Take the Outer Drive to 16 Lake Street. I'm going to meet a friend of mine who's also a friend of yours.

BIGGER. Friend of mine!

THE BLACK RAT. Shhh!

MARY. "You'll understand it better bye and bye." Isn't there a song like that your people sing?

BIGGER. Yessum.

MARY. If anyone should ask you, then I went to the University, see, Bigger?

BIGGER. Yessum.

MARY. There he is! Stop the car!

(Lights.)

Scene Twenty
With Buddy

(Lights.)

(Earlier.)

BIGGER. Stop the crap! What you say to me?

BUDDY. If you not nervous then why you worried about Gus not showing up?

BIGGER. You shouldn't even be here –

BUDDY. You made such a big deal –

BIGGER. This is grown men's work –

BUDDY. You nervous, Bigger?

BIGGER. Gus nervous. You nervous –

BUDDY. If we don't today, we can do it tomorrow –

BIGGER. Tomorrow's Sunday, fool –!

THE BLACK RAT. Stay calm.

BUDDY. There you go again, Bigger! Just like when Ma snap at you! You *are* nervous!

(**BIGGER** *grabs* **BUDDY.**)

Turn me loose, Bigger!

BIGGER. I'm not nervous!

(Lights.)

Scene Twenty One
With Mary

(Lights.)

(Later.)

*(A young white man enters. At once **BIGGER** recognizes him as **JAN** from the **NEWSREEL**.)*

JAN. Don't be nervous. Mary told me all about you. How are you, Bigger?

BIGGER. Fine, suh.

JAN. Come on and shake.

MARY. Shake his hand, Bigger. Go on.

BIGGER. Yessum.

> *(**BIGGER** extends a limp palm, they grip hands.)*

JAN. I'm a friend of Mary's.

BIGGER. Yessuh.

> *(**BIGGER** tries to pull away.)*

JAN. Oh no, Bigger. Don't let go.

BIGGER. Yessuh.

JAN. And don't say "sir" to me. I'll call you Bigger and you'll call me Jan. How's that?

MARY. It's all right, Bigger. Jan *means* it.

THE BLACK RAT. What do these people want?

> *(**BIGGER** tries again to pull his hand away.)*

JAN. Don't pull your hand away. We are officially comrades.

> *(**JAN** lets go of **BIGGER**'s hand.)*

Scoot over. Let me drive awhile. Don't be scared.

(Lights.)

Scene Twenty Two
With Buddy

(Lights.)

(Earlier.)

BIGGER. I ain't scared!

(**BIGGER** *unknowingly squeezes* **BUDDY** *hard.*)

BUDDY. I can't breathe!

THE BLACK RAT. Don't rob Blum's.

(Lights.)

Scene Twenty Three
With Mary

(Lights.)

(Later.)

BIGGER. Don't – I'll – I'll just get out the car and wait for you here, suh–

JAN. No, "suh!" And no getting out the car. Stay in and move over. Mary come get in the front too –

MARY. Move over, Bigger. Right between me and Jan. A Bigger sandwich.

(**BIGGER** *is now wedged between* **JAN** *and* **MARY**.)

Say. I've never been this close to a Negro before…

THE BLACK RAT. Can smell her hair, feel her thigh –

JAN. Bigger, where can we get a good meal on the South Side?

MARY. We want one of those places where colored people eat, some place that's got some good liquor.

BIGGER. Well, there's Ernie's Kitchen Shack at 47th and Indiana.

THE BLACK RAT. Bessie will be there –

JAN. Do they have anything stronger than beer there?

MARY. Yes, like a fifth of rum?

JAN. Mary, aren't you still hungover from last night?

MARY. And I can handle a bit more tonight! Packing my trunk and leaving for Detroit early in the morning, it's my last night to be decadent.

JAN. So be decadent!

(**JAN** *takes out a flask.* **MARY** *snatches it, swigs.*)

MARY. Want some Bigger?

THE BLACK RAT. Goddamn these damn people.

JAN. Go on. There's plenty.

MARY. You aren't scared –?

JAN. It's just liquor –

MARY. You're scared?

(Lights.)

Scene Twenty Four
With Buddy

(Lights.)

(Earlier.)

THE BLACK RAT. Don't do it. Offer him a game. Call it a day. Don't rob Blums.

> *(***BIGGER*** whirls and kicks ***BUDDY*** hard. Laughing.)*

GUS. What you kick me for?

THE BLACK RAT. Dummy.

BIGGER. 'Cause Gus late.

BUDDY. He ain't late.

BIGGER. Shut up, Buddy! He *is* late!

BUDDY. It's only ten minutes to 3.

BIGGER. I ain't no fool, Buddy!

THE BLACK RAT. Aw, leave 'im alone.

BUDDY. Coward.

> *(***BIGGER*** flicks his switchblade at ***BUDDY***'s face.)*

BIGGER. Lick it. Lick it, I said!

BUDDY. Hey – I – I – I'm sorry Gus is late –

THE BLACK RAT. Put that switchblade away –

BIGGER. You think I'm playing?

BUDDY. Sorry Gus is late –

THE BLACK RAT. Ain't you scared 'im enough –?

BIGGER. Shut your mouth!

BUDDY. I'm sorry – I'm the coward, see-Please don't hurt me – don't hurt me –

BIGGER. Lick it goddamnit!

> *(***BUDDY***'s lips move toward the knife.)*

THE BLACK RAT. Simmer down!

(**BUDDY** *pushes* **BIGGER** *into the pool table and runs.*)

BIGGER. Push me into the pool table?

(**BUDDY** *grabs a cue stick.*)

Put that down!

BUDDY. Pull a knife on me?! I'll kill you!

(**BUDDY** *lunges towards* **BIGGER**. **BIGGER** *cowers in fear.*)

Aw! Look at you! Cry baby ass!

BIGGER. Shut up!

BUDDY. Black bastard.

BIGGER. Go to hell!

BUDDY.	**THE BLACK RAT.**
Scared.	Scared.

(*Lights.*)

Scene Twenty Five
With Mary

(Lights.)

(Later.)

(The **DALTON***'s Car.* **BIGGER** *now slightly intoxicated.)*

JAN. Scared? He drinks like a fish!

MARY. Like a fish!

JAN. Mary make that fish face!

MARY. Only if you make yours first!

(They make fish faces, laughing.)

(They ride.)

Oh, how I want to see how your people live! I've been to England, France, and Mexico, but I don't know how people live ten blocks from me. Were you born in one of those houses?

BIGGER. Born in Mississippi.

MARY. Once I saw a couple and their three young children in one of those houses, unclothed.

JAN. Oh my.

MARY. Yes! My curiosity about Negroes has been aroused ever since. They're human after all, all twelve million of them. Bigger, you live nearby with your mother, brother, and sister?

BIGGER. Yeah.

JAN. Where's your father?

BIGGER.	**THE BLACK RAT**.
…Dead.	Dead.

MARY. Of course he is. Now, how was he killed?

JAN. Mary! How did he die?

BIGGER. He got killed in a riot when I was a kid.

MARY. A kid? How old?

BIGGER. Eight.

JAN. How do you feel about it?

BIGGER. ...I don't know. He dead He –

BIGGER.	**THE BLACK RAT.**
...Dead.	Dead.

(Lights.)

Scene Twenty Six
With Himself

(Lights.)

(Earlier.)

(BIGGER *whirls around to see,* **THE BLACK RAT** *reflected in the remaining cracked pieces of* **BIGGER***'s reflection.* **THE BLACK RAT** *watches* **BIGGER** *with an almost amused contempt and pity.)*

(BIGGER *sees himself in the mirror as* **THE BLACK RAT***. They [he] lock eyes [with himself].)*

BIGGER. She's – she's – she's – dead?

THE BLACK RAT. Dead.

BIGGER.	**THE BLACK RAT.**
They will kill me.	They will kill me.

*(***BIGGER** *starts to hyperventilate.)*

BIGGER. I've got to get out of here –

THE BLACK RAT. Calm down. Light a fag.

BIGGER. Where did I put –?

THE BLACK RAT. In my pocket. Upper right.

*(***BIGGER** *reaches to his own pocket. Matches appear.)*

I put it there before Ma said grace. Or was it after I beat the crap out of Buddy. Light me up.

*(***BIGGER** *takes a match. His hands shake.)*

My hands are trembling.

BIGGER. I killed a white woman – I'm black – They will kill me.

THE BLACK RAT. What am I going to say to 'em?

BIGGER. ...I could say I had driven Mary home and had left her at the side door –

THE BLACK RAT. But what about the communist?

BIGGER. Jan will say he left us together in the car at Forty-sixth and Cottage.

THE BLACK RAT. But I would tell them it was not true.

BIGGER. Is not my word as good as his?

THE BLACK RAT. Yes. After all, isn't Jan a Red?

(Lights.)

Scene Twenty Seven
With Mary

(Lights.)

(Earlier.)

(**BIGGER** *now feels the effects of liquor.*)

JAN. And that's what we Communists are fighting.

THE BLACK RAT. So he is a Red.

JAN. Don't you think we could stop things like what happened to your father?

(**BIGGER** *swigs.*)

BIGGER. I don't know. There's a lot of white people in the world.

THE BLACK RAT. Slow the liquor, boy.

JAN. Like those Scottsboro boys, don't you think we did a good job in keeping 'em from killing them?

THE BLACK RAT. I'd rather have died than what they got. Don't say that.

MARY. Say, isn't it glorious tonight?

JAN. God, yes! This is a beautiful world, Bigger. After the revolution, it'll be ours. And then, there'll be no rich and no poor, no white and no Negro –

MARY. Jan, do you know many Negroes?

JAN. I don't know any very well. But you'll meet them when you join the Party.

MARY. Glorious!

JAN. I've got some pamphlets I want to share with you. Please read them. Please. We'd like to be friends of yours.

MARY. He'll read them. After all, you're fighting for him. His people. The Negroes! They have so much emotion! And their songs! Say, Bigger, can you sing?

BIGGER. I can't sing.

JAN. Are we almost there?

BIGGER. End of the next block.

MARY. *(she sings)*

> SWING LOW, SWEET CHARIOT/COMING FER TO CARRY ME
> HOME.../

JAN. Come on, Bigger, you'll get use to us, help us sing.

BIGGER. I can't sing.

MARY/JAN.

> SWING LOW, SWEET CHARIOT/COMING FER TO CARRY ME
> HOME.../

MARY. We seem strange to you, don't we, Bigger?

BIGGER. Oh, no'm.

MARY/JAN.

> COMING FER TO CARRY ME HOME.../

> > (**JAN** *passes the flask. All three sip as they exit the car.*)

> > *(Lights.)*

Scene Twenty Eight
With Himself

(Lights.)

(Later.)

BIGGER. Say I'd carried them home and that Jan didn't leave at Forty-sixth Street – He rode with us.

THE BLACK RAT. Jan had come to the house. Mary asked me to leave the car in the driveway and go with her to her room to get the trunk – and Jan was with us. And I got the trunk and took it to the basement and when I'd gone I'd left Mary and Jan sitting in the car –

BIGGER. – Kissing. Reds'd do anything. Didn't the papers say so?

THE BLACK RAT. Make them think Jan did it.

BIGGER. Make them think Jan did it.

(Lights.)

Scene Twenty Nine
With Daltons

(Lights.)

(Later.)

(The **DALTONS***'.)*

MRS. DALTON. Just got a wire from Detroit saying Mary never got there. What happened?! You left the car in the driveway?

BIGGER. Yessum. Miss Dalton told me to leave it.

MRS. DALTON. Mary told you to leave the car?

BIGGER. Yessum.

MRS. DALTON. …And you took the trunk to the station this morning, didn't you?

BIGGER. Yessum.

MRS. DALTON. …You'd better go to the station and pick up her trunk then.

BIGGER. Yessum –

MRS. DALTON. – She took you to her room to get the trunk?

BIGGER. Yessum –

THE BLACK RAT. Make them think Jan did it.

BIGGER. …*They* went up –

MRS. DALTON. They? Someone was with her?

BIGGER. Yessum… A gentleman.

MRS. DALTON. A gentleman?

BIGGER. Yessum. A gentleman.

(Lights.)

Scene Thirty
With Daltons

(Lights.)

(Later.)

(MR. BRITTEN.)

MR. BRITTEN. And what did this gentleman say to you?! Relax, boy. I ain't the police. Just a Dick.

BIGGER. Suh?

MRS. DALTON. A private investigator my husband has hired. Easy, Mr. Britten. This boy is trying to get a new start.

MR. BRITTEN. They're all just niggers to me, mam. I'll debrief Mr. Dalton when I'm done here.

MRS. DALTON Thank you, Mr. Britten.

(She exits.)

BRITTEN Now, spit it out, boy.

BIGGER. ...He talked about the Communists –

MR. BRITTEN. I knew it. Did he ask you to join?

BIGGER. He...told me that some day there wouldn't be no rich folks and no poor folks –

MR. BRITTEN. Jesus, this Jan sounds like my old lady. Yeah?

BIGGER. That a black man would have a chance –

MR. BRITTEN. A chance? What could a negro possibly do? Keep talking, boy.

BIGGER. That there would be no more lynchings –

MR. BRITTEN. Genius putting that in your head! And what was the girl saying?

BIGGER. She agreed with 'im.

MR. BRITTEN. Did this fellow Jan say he would let you meet some white women if you joined the Reds?

BIGGER. Nawsuh.

MR. BRITTEN. Now after you left the restaurant and drove them around the park, did Jan lay the girl. Did Jan lay the girl?!

BIGGER. I don't know, suh. They was back there kissing and going on.

MR. BRITTEN. They were drunk, weren't they?

BIGGER. Yessuh. They'd been drinking. A lot.

> (**BIGGER** *lowers his eyes, acting.*)

THE BLACK RAT. Bravo.

MR. BRITTEN. Now how drunk was Miss Dalton?

> (*Lights.*)

Scene Thirty One
With Bessie

(Lights.)

(Later.)

(BESSIE's *house.)*

BESSIE. I saw you last night at Ernie's with your drunk white friends.

BIGGER. Aw, Bessie. They wasn't my friends. I work for 'em.

BESSIE. And you eat chicken and drink Rum with 'em. I thought maybe you was 'shamed of me getting my after work drink in my dirty work clothes. Just come from cleaning my white woman's house and you sitting there, with that crazy white gal all dressed in silk and satin. You ain't even speak to me.

BIGGER. I did. And I been thinking hard about you. Been missing you.

BESSIE. You just growled and waved your hand. Too busy looking at that old white gal batting her eyes at you, I reckon. My hair wasn't pressed but I still smelled clean. You don't love me no more.

BIGGER. The hell I don't.

> **(BIGGER** *grabs* **BESSIE**'s *arm, pulling her towards him, and kisses her long and hard. She does not respond. He reaches into his pocket drawing the roll of bills.)*

BESSIE. Lord, Bigger! Where you get this money from? You ain't got into nothing, is you?

BIGGER. You going to kiss me now, honey?

> **(BESSIE** *gives in, kissing him, and she draws* **BIGGER** *to the bed. He gives her the wad. She counts it.)*

BESSIE. A hundred and twenty-five dollars? You going to buy me something?

THE BLACK RAT. She only wants to get drunk.

BESSIE. You love me?

BIGGER. Sure.

BESSIE. Bigger, where you get this money from?

BIGGER. What do it matter?

> (**BIGGER** *kisses* **BESSIE** *again, hard. He places his hands on her breasts, just as he had placed them on* **MARY***'s the night before. She opens her blouse. He nestles his face in her bosom.*)

You smell good.

THE BLACK RAT. Like gin and bleach.

BIGGER. Get close to me.

> (**BIGGER** *pulls* **BESSIE** *closer to him. He kisses her.*)

BESSIE. You feel different.

BIGGER. You feel good.

BESSIE. Was you with that white girl?

> (*Lights.*)

Scene Thirty Two
With Daltons

(Lights.)

(Earlier.)

JAN. No I wasn't with Miss Dalton last night. Now come on. Let's get this over with. What do you really want?

MR. BRITTEN. Oh! You're one of those tough Reds, hunh?

JAN. What do you want?!

MR. BRITTEN. Nothing. My boy is out of college, my old lady is out her mind, and knocking your filthy kind down is what I need for promotion. Bigger, is this the man Miss Dalton brought here last night?

THE BLACK RAT. Yessuh.

BIGGER. Yessuh.

JAN. You didn't bring me here, Bigger! What're you making this boy lie for? What is this?

MR. BRITTEN. Where's Miss Dalton?

JAN. Honestly, sir, I'm confused. I called her this morning but she was already gone. She's in Detroit.

MR. BRITTEN. You didn't give these pamphlets to this boy last night?

> (**BRITTEN** *pulls the pamphlets from his coat pocket.*
> **JAN** *shrugs his shoulders, smiles.*)

JAN. All right. I saw her. So what?

MR. BRITTEN. And the boy told us you and Miss Dalton were stinking drunk last night, weren't you?

> *(Lights.)*

Scene Thirty Three
With Daltons

(Lights.)

(Earlier.)

THE BLACK RAT. Well, she couldn't hardly stand up, suh.

BIGGER. Well, she couldn't hardly stand up, suh. When we got home, Mr. Jan had to lift her up the steps.

MR. BRITTEN. What else happened?

BIGGER. Well…it was Mr. Jan who told me to take the trunk down and not put the car away.

MR. BRITTEN. Why didn't you tell us this before, Bigger?

BIGGER. He told me not to, suh.

MR. BRITTEN. What else did this Jan say about the Party?

THE BLACK RAT. Where's he going with this?

BIGGER. Suh?

MR. BRITTEN. Aw, come on boy! Don't stall! Tell me what he said about the Party!

BIGGER. It wasn't no party, mister. He made me sit at his table and he bought chicken and told me to eat.

MR. BRITTEN. What unit are you in?

BIGGER. Suh?

MR. BRITTEN. Come on, Comrade, aren't you a Communist!?

THE BLACK RAT.	**BIGGER**.
Goddamn!	Nawsuh! You got me wrong. I ain't never fooled around with them folks. Miss Dalton and Mr. Jan was the first ones I ever met, so help me God!

(**BRITTEN** *rams* **BIGGER** *against the wall.*)

MR. BRITTEN. You *are* a Communist –!

MR. BRITTEN`.   BESSIE. *(offstage)*

You goddamn black   You goddamn black
sonofabitch!   sonofabitch −!

(**BRITTEN** *jerks from his pocket* **JAN**'s *pamphlets.*)

(Lights.)

Scene Thirty Four
With Bessie

(Lights.)

(Later.)

BESSIE. Was you with that white girl?!

BIGGER. Naw. Now come here, girl.

BESSIE. Just can't treat me any old way, Bigger Thomas.

BIGGER. The hell I cain't!

THE BLACK RAT. You need her. Sweet talk her.

BIGGER. Reach in. Take my flask.

*(***BESSIE*** does.)*

I gave you the liquor. Now give me what I want.

*(She succumbs. ***BIGGER*** mounts her.)*

(Grunts. Groans.)

(Lights.)

Scene Thirty Five
With Himself

(Earlier.)

(Grunts. Groans.)

(Lights.)

*(**BIGGER** pulls **MARY**'s trunk. An idea.)*

BIGGER. I could, I could put her in the trunk! She is small. Yes. Put her in the trunk.

*(**BIGGER** goes to dead **MARY**. He stops.)*

THE BLACK RAT. Well. Go on, touch her.

BIGGER. What if she screams?

THE BLACK RAT. Scared of a dead woman? Trembling, sweating, breathing hard, like a sissy!

BIGGER. I ain't no sissy! I killed the bitch didn't I?

THE BLACK RAT. Then get it done. Save your life.

*(**BIGGER** shoves **MARY**'s body in the trunk. He and **THE BLACK RAT** both pull, push, tug.)*

BIGGER. Too much. Too heavy.

*(The furnace appears before **BIGGER**.)*

I – I could, I – I could put her, I could – put her in the furnace. I will burn her!

THE BLACK RAT. Nothing left behind. Good thinking. Put the trunk away first.

(They resume pushing, pulling, tugging, the trunk.)

Push it –

THE BLACK RAT.	**BESSIE**.
– Harder – harder –	– Harder – harder –

(Grunts. Groans.)

(Lights.)

Scene Thirty Six
With Bessie

(Later.)

(Grunts. Groans.)

BESSIE. – Harder – harder – You – you – love me – Bigger? – You love me?

BIGGER. – Sure –

BESSIE. – Say "yes –" "Yes, I love you –"

(He doesn't answer. Climactic sex sounds.)

(Lights. **BESSIE** *sips from the flask.)*

Want some? Not much left.

BIGGER. Naw.

(Silence.)

BESSIE. So…

BIGGER. So.

BESSIE. …Where you say you working at?

BIGGER. Over on Drexel. 4600 block.

BESSIE. I used to work there, not far from where them Loeb folks lived.

BIGGER. Loeb?

BESSIE. You remember hearing people talk about Loeb and Leopold. The ones who killed that boy and then tried to get money from his family by sending letters for ransom –

*(***BIGGER** *sits up in bed.)*

THE BLACK RAT. Ransom?

BESSIE.	**MR. BRITTEN.**
What's wrong with you?	What's wrong with you?

(Lights.)

Scene Thirty Seven
With Daltons

(Lights.)

(Earlier.)

MR. BRITTEN. Tell the truth. Weren't you and Miss Dalton drunk?!

JAN. We just had a little to drink –

MR. BRITTEN. Where is she?

JAN. If she's not in Detroit, then I don't know where she is.

MR. BRITTEN. You brought her home about two?

JAN. ...Yeah.

MR. BRITTEN. You told the boy to take her trunk down to the basement?

JAN. Say, what is this?

MR. BRITTEN. Where's their daughter, Mr. Erlone? She was drunk last night when you brought her here –

JAN. I – I didn't come here last night.

MR. BRITTEN. You didn't tell the boy to take the trunk down?

JAN. Hell no! Who says I did? I left the car and took a trolley home. ...Where's Mary?

(Lights.)

Scene Thirty Eight
With Bessie

(Lights.)

(Later.)

BIGGER. I don't know where she is.

BESSIE. You ain't acting right. You hurt that girl?

BIGGER. Naw.

BESSIE. Then where is she? She in a hospital? Run off with that Communist? Stole her daddy's loot, what?

BIGGER. I don't know.

BESSIE. You hurt her.

BIGGER. I didn't.

BESSIE. You did.

BIGGER. I didn't!

BESSIE. Bigger, what's happened to you? She dead?

BIGGER. Don't you trust me, baby?

BESSIE. Where's that girl, Bigger?

BIGGER. I don't know.

BESSIE. If you hurt her you'll hurt me –

THE BLACK RAT. Tell her. Bonnie and Clyde. Leopold and Loeb. Bigger and Bessie –

BESSIE. I see it all over you.

BIGGER. You don't see me.

BESSIE. I see you. Smell you too.

BIGGER. Aw...forget the girl!

THE BLACK RAT. First time I ever did something. Tell her.

BIGGER. I ain't killed nobody!

BESSIE. I ain't say you did. But you just did. Where the hell is that white girl, Bigger?!

(Lights.)

Scene Thirty Nine
With Daltons

(Lights.)

(Earlier.)

MR. BRITTEN. We're waiting for you to tell us.

JAN. D – d – d – didn't she go to Detroit?

MR. BRITTEN. No.

JAN. Bigger, why did you tell these men I came here?

THE BLACK RAT. Don't answer.

MR. BRITTEN. Leave 'im alone! Come on, Erlone, you've been lying ever since you've been here. Where's Miss Dalton?

JAN. Is this a game?

MR. BRITTEN. Listen, Mr. Erlone, Mary's the only child they've got. Tell her to come back. Or you bring her back. The Dalton's will make it all right with you... How much money can they pay you –

JAN. Pay me –?

JAN.	**BESSIE.** *(offstage)*
You sonofa –!	You sonofa –!

(Lights.)

Scene Forty
With Bessie

(Lights.)

(Earlier.)

BESSIE. – Bitch! Tell me!

BIGGER. Awright Goddamnit! Yeah I killed her! I killed the white girl!

(Silence.)

You got to help me.

BESSIE. For Chrissakes!

BIGGER. Don't be afraid of me!

(**BIGGER** *raises his hand to slap her.* **BESSIE** *cowers.*)

BIGGER.	**JAN**. *(os)*
Don't be afraid of me.	– Don't be afraid of me.

(Lights.)

Scene Forty One
With Daltons

(Lights.)

(Earlier.)

(**JAN** *is there. He comes towards* **BIGGER**, **BIGGER** *backs away.*)

JAN. – I'm not going to hurt you. What's all this about, Bigger? I haven't done anything to you have I? Where's Mary?

THE BLACK RAT. Keep walking.

BIGGER. I don't want to talk to you –

JAN. Listen, if these people are bothering you, just tell me. Don't be scared. Let's go somewhere and get a cup of coffee and talk this thing over –

BIGGER. I don't want to talk to you... Go'way –

JAN. But Bigger, what have I done to you –

(**BIGGER** *draws his gun.*)

For God's sakes man! What're you doing? Don't shoot – I haven't bothered you – Don't –

BIGGER. *(near scream)*	**BESSIE.** *(near scream)*
Leave me alone!	Leave me alone!

(Lights.)

Scene Forty Two
With Bessie

(Lights.)

(Later.)

*(***BIGGER*** *and* ***BESSIE***.*)*

BESSIE. Please, Bigger! I don't want to help you, don't make me do it, they'll catch us, God knows they will!

THE BLACK RAT. Can't leave her behind to snitch –

BIGGER. You got to help me! Look at me girl.

BESSIE. Look at you?! I see inside your dark, beady eyes. Still I say to myself, be with him, he good!

BIGGER. I got a plan, Bessie –

BESSIE. Tell you about my baby –

BIGGER. You gonna hide in one of them abandoned buildings –

BESSIE. How he like a nip from my flask –

BIGGER. They gonna drop the money –

BESSIE. How I pick him up that day –

BIGGER. You wait for a sign from me –

BESSIE. And he ain't breathin' –

BIGGER. Then you grab the money –

BESSIE. I told you that!

BIGGER. Then we can hideout –

BESSIE. Wish I'd never met you. Wish both of us died before we was born. Where's that goddamn flask?!

BIGGER. Pipe down! Or I'll…–

BESSIE. You'll what?

BIGGER. – I'll…I'll – k – k – k –

(Lights.)

Scene Forty Three
With Himself

(Lights.)

(Later.)

(BESSIE's place. BIGGER takes the pencil into his trembling hands. He writes.)

THE BLACK RAT. No! You won't kill her. Say "I won't kill her." Say "I want you to put – "

BIGGER. "I want you to put – "

THE BLACK RAT. "Ten thousand – "

BIGGER. Naw. Not "I." We. "We want you to put…"

THE BLACK RAT. That's better.

BIGGER. *(writing)* "…We got your daughter. She is safe… She wants to come home… Don't go to the police if you want your daughter back safe…"

THE BLACK RAT. Naw. "…If you want your daughter back alive – "

BIGGER. "Get ten thousand in 5 and 10 bills and put it in a shoe box…"

THE BLACK RAT. That's good!

BIGGER. "…Do what this letter say or…"

THE BLACK RAT. "Or…or… –"

BIGGER. "Or…"

(He writes. He finishes, puts the pencil down.)

I done it.

THE BLACK RAT. Don't forget to sign it with the other hand so they don't know.

BIGGER. Oh yeah.

> *(He then signs the letter with his opposite hand and seals it.)*

THE BLACK RAT. The Loeb brothers ain't got nothing on me.

> *(Flashbulbs.)*

Scene Forty Four
With Daltons

(Later.)

(The flashing lights of newspapermen snapping photos at the **DALTONS***'.)*

MR. BRITTEN. ...Yes, gentlemen, tell the kidnappers through your papers the Dalton's will do everything they ask. They'll pay as they've been instructed. They shall not call in the police. Tell them to please return their daughter...Oh, and the signature on the ransom note? It's signed, "Red."

(Flashbulbs flash.)

Scene Forty Five
With Daltons

(Lights.)

(Later.)

*(**MR. BRITTEN** walks over to **BIGGER**, surrounded by press. **THE WHITE CAT** eyes **THE BLACK RAT**.)*

MR. BRITTEN. C'mere. Who do you think did it, Mike?

BIGGER. My name ain't Mike.

MR. BRITTEN. Easy, boy, it's a figure o' speech.

*(**THE WHITE CAT** sits on **BIGGER**'s lap.)*

THE BLACK RAT. Damn cat! Get off!

MR. BRITTEN. If there's a spook in the room, he's surely the one who did it! Even the cat thinks so!

*(Laughter. The press start snapping pictures of **THE WHITE CAT** in **BIGGER**'s lap.)*

*(**MRS. DALTON** enters.)*

MRS. DALTON. Bigger, there's not enough heat upstairs. You'd better clean those ashes out and make a better fire.

THE BLACK RAT.	**BIGGER**.
Yessum.	Yessum.

*(**BIGGER** doesn't move.)*

MRS. DALTON. You better do what I say, Bigger. Don't be afraid. Nobody's going to hurt you.

MR. BRITTEN. Aw, he doesn't know anything, Mrs. Dalton. He's a dumb cluck. Is that right, boy?

BIGGER. Yessuh. A dumb cluck.

(Lights.)

Scene Forty Six
With Himself

(Lights.)

(Earlier.)

(The **DALTONS***'.)*

THE BLACK RAT. Not a dumb cluck, c'mon boy, think!

BIGGER. I've got to burn this body!

THE BLACK RAT. Calm down. The old lady'll hear. Got to get the body in –

> *(***BIGGER*** opens the furnace door.* **THE BLACK RAT** *opens the trunk.* **BIGGER** *picks up* **MARY***'s body. They try to push* **MARY***'s body in the furnace.)*

BIGGER. Dammit! The shoulders are stuck.

THE BLACK RAT. Come on. Push! Push!

> *(They try. Shoulders in. But –)*

Goddamnit, the head! It won't go in –! Cut that bitch's precious white throat.

> *(***BIGGER*** reaches into his pocket, pulls out his knife.)*

BIGGER. Wait! It'll bleed.

THE BLACK RAT. Shut up thinking and cut! No time. Got to save my life.

BIGGER. There'll be blood everywhere and they'll see it and they'll know and –

THE BLACK RAT. Am I some scared, dumb, mindless, rodent letting them decide who I am?

BIGGER. Newspaper! I saw newspaper in that corner.

THE BLACK RAT. Lay it down here.

> *(***BIGGER*** does.)*

Now whack it hard, Captain Pilot.

> *(***BIGGER*** tries.)*

BIGGER. Shoot! I've hit a bone!

THE BLACK RAT. Keep trying –! Man the flight.

> (**BIGGER** *keeps whacking as he talks.*)

BIGGER.	THE BLACK RAT.
I am a murderer. A Negro murderer. A Black murderer.	I am a murderer. A Negro murderer. A Black murderer.

THE BLACK RAT. I killed a white woman! Talking to me that way and letting Jan hold my hand and sitting next to me with your thigh touching mine and making me drink and making me bring you home and you're drunk. Don't you understand they would fire me if they find me in your room. You want me to lose my job? You made me do it. I had to – I had to –

THE BLACK RAT.	BIGGER.
I hate you –	I hate you!

BIGGER. You rich white precious bitch!

> (**MARY**'s *head still hangs on.*)
>
> (*A hatchet appears.*)
>
> (**BIGGER** *picks it up in his black hands.*)
>
> (*Chop.*)
>
> (*Black out into –*)
>
> (*Coughing.*)

Scene Forty Seven
With Daltons

(Later.)

(Thick, black smoke filling the air.)

MR. BRITTEN. You better do something about those ashes, boy!

MRS. DALTON. The fire can't get any air!

BIGGER. Yessum.

> (**BIGGER** *grabs the shovel and just holds onto it. They are really coughing now.*)

THE BLACK RAT. Do it. Or they will know.

MR. BRITTEN. Say, you!

MRS. DALTON. Get some of those ashes out of there!

MR. BRITTEN. What're you trying to do! Smother us?! I can't see! The smoke's got my eyes!

BIGGER. I'm gettin' 'em out.

THE BLACK RAT. Move!

> (**BIGGER** *still does not move.*)

THE BLACK RAT. You black fool!

MR. BRITTEN. Here! Give me that shovel! I'll h – h – h – elp you!

BIGGER. Nawsuh. I – I – I can do it.

MR. BRITTEN. C – come on! L – let go!

THE BLACK RAT. Let go.

BIGGER. Yessuh. Not a problem suh.

> (**BIGGER** *lets go of the shovel.*)

MR. BRITTEN. Open the frontdoor! I'm choking!

> *(Someone opens a door.* **MR. BRITTEN** *continues emptying the ashes. Suddenly we hear a draft, a suck of air. The vent is now clear.)*

MR. BRITTEN. There was a hell of a lot of ashes in there, Bigger. You shouldn't let it get that way.

BIGGER. Yessuh.

MR. BRITTEN. What's the matter, boy?

BIGGER. Nothing.

> (**BRITTEN** *looks down at the ashes.*)

MR. BRITTEN. Say, come here, Mrs. Dalton

> (**BIGGER** *tiptoes, looks over their shoulders into the ashes.*)

MRS. DALTON. *(sniffing the air)* That's just some garbage we're burning –

MR. BRITTEN. It's... My God!

THE BLACK RAT. You dumb –

MRS. DALTON. Wait, let me feel that...

MR. BRITTEN. It's bone...

> (**MR. BRITTEN** *hands her a charred object.*)

THE BLACK RAT. Stupid –

MRS DALTON. It's Mary's earring...

MR. BRITTEN. It's the girl!

THE BLACK RAT. Nigger.

> *(Unseen by anyone,* **BIGGER** *tiptoes up the steps.)*

> *(A window appears before him.)*

Fly.

> (**BIGGER** *runs, leaps out the window.*)

> *(White out.)*

FLIGHT

Scene Forty Eight
Rat Standoff

(In the white.)

(Later.)

*(***BIGGER*** *falls facedown in the snow as snow falls all around him.)*

*(***BIGGER*** *and* **THE BLACK RAT** *both struggle to get up.)*

BIGGER. Can't – fly.

THE BLACK RAT. Run.

BIGGER. Can't run –

THE BLACK RAT. Walk.

BIGGER. Can't walk –

THE BLACK RAT. Crawl.

BIGGER. Can't crawl –

THE BLACK RAT. Move.

BIGGER. Can't move. Dead.

THE BLACK RAT. Try.

BIGGER. Can't –

THE BLACK RAT. Got to –

BIGGER. Too much snow.

THE BLACK RAT. Move!

BIGGER. White everywhere –

THE BLACK RAT. It's just snow.

BIGGER. *Whites* everywhere!

THE BLACK RAT. Free!

BIGGER. Ain't free.

THE BLACK RAT. Goddamnit, Bigger, run!

*(**BIGGER** picks himself up off the ground and runs for his [their] life.)*

(Lights.)

Scene Forty Nine
With Bessie

(Later.)

(**THE BLACK RAT** *and* **BIGGER** *arrive at* **BESSIE**'s.)

BIGGER. Turn off the light.

BESSIE. Bigger! What's happened?

BIGGER. Turn off the light! It's all off.

BESSIE. I don't have to do it?

BIGGER. They found the girl.

BESSIE. Did you send that letter asking for that money?

BIGGER. …

BESSIE. They'll come for me. They'll know you did it and they'll talk to your ma and brother and they'll come for me now for sure.

BIGGER. If you don't act better'n this, I'll just leave.

BESSIE. Naw, naw… Bigger!

BIGGER. Then shut up!

BESSIE. Did you kiss her?

BIGGER. What?

BESSIE. Did you kiss her? Touch her?

BIGGER. Naw! Well…

BESSIE. Goddamnit, Bigger –

BIGGER. But what do it matter now?

BESSIE. You oughtn't've killed her, honey. Don't you see? They'll say –

BIGGER.	**THE BLACK RAT**.
What?	What?

BESSIE. They'll… They'll say you raped her…

THE BLACK RAT. She right.

BIGGER. Get your hat and coat on. And get them blankets and quilts. We got to get out of here.

(Lights.)

Scene Fifty
With Bessie

(Lights.)

(Later.)

(An abandoned building.)

BIGGER. Unroll these blankets.

BESSIE. I take orders from whites, not you.

BIGGER. Oh you smart, now? Spread 'em out. Where's the money?

BESSIE. Ninety dollars in my dress pocket –

BIGGER. Only Ninety?

BESSIE. Payed my rent. Bought more liquor. Goddamnit, Bigger! I been a fool, just a blind dumb drunk black fool following your dumb black ass.

THE BLACK RAT. There's two bricks in that doorway –

BIGGER. Snap out of it, girl. Here. Lay down.

BESSIE. I need a drink. You got the bottle?

BIGGER. In my pocket. You smell good.

THE BLACK RAT. Check the doors.

BESSIE. Feel like I'll never get warm.

BIGGER. Get closer to me.

THE BLACK RAT. Keep watch. They're coming.

BESSIE. You so hot. You got a fever?

BIGGER. Undo that button –

BESSIE. Don't touch me there –

BIGGER. I – I have to –

BESSIE. Too rough –

BIGGER. Can't help it –

BESSIE. Please, baby –

BIGGER. Cannot help it now – I'm sorry, I have to –

THE BLACK RAT. Help it.

BIGGER. Can't help it.

THE BLACK RAT. Help it.

BIGGER. Sorry!

THE BLACK RAT. Help it!

BIGGER. Turnin' off the light. Can't help it –!

BESSIE.	**THE BLACK RAT**.
Bigger don't –!	Bigger don't –!

(**BIGGER** *turns off the flashlight.*)

(*Blackout.*)

(*Groans.*)

(*Grunts.*)

(*Tustling.*)

(*Protests.*)

(*Tattered Resolution.*)

(*A Long Silence.*)

BIGGER. …She sleep?

THE BLACK RAT. Can't leave her here and I can't take her with.

BIGGER. Hope she's sleep.

THE BLACK RAT. Those two bricks when we walked in, where were they –?

BIGGER. Shouldn't have told her.

THE BLACK RAT. I had to tell her.

BIGGER. How could I know they'd find that white girl's bones so quick?

THE BLACK RAT. Can't leave her and I can't take her with.

BIGGER. She's sleep.

THE BLACK RAT. Can't use the gun, too much noise –

BIGGER. Can't leave her and I can't take her with –

THE BLACK RAT. Dump it down the air-shaft. Nobody will find it –

BIGGER. What if it smells?

THE BLACK RAT. Cannot leave her and I cannot take her with –

BIGGER. Cannot leave her and I cannot take her with –

THE BLACK RAT. She will be crying all the time, blaming me, wanting whiskey to help her forget –

BIGGER. Her breathing is deep. Peaceful.

THE BLACK RAT. Cannot leave her –

BIGGER. – And I can't take her with –!

THE BLACK RAT. It's my life against hers –!

BIGGER.	**THE BLACK RAT.**
Can't leave her and I can't take her with –!	Can't leave her and I can't take her with –!

THE BLACK RAT. Where's that brick?

(**BIGGER** *grabs a brick poised to strike.*)

(*Lights.*)

(**BIGGER**'*s mind: The glare of the furnace.* **MRS. DALTON** *and* **MR. BRITTEN** *and others look on, judging.*)

MR. BRITTEN. It's bone.

MRS. DALTON. It's Mary's earring.

ALL. It's the girl!

(*Lights.*)

(**BIGGER** *swoops down with the brick down to where* **BESSIE**'*s head must be* –

(*Thud / blackout*)

(*She moans.*)

(*Thud.*)

(*She moans.*)

(*Thud.*)

(*Thud. Thud.*)

(*Thud Thud Thud… Silence.*)

(The sound of blankets and clothes being wrapped up.)

THE BLACK RAT. Where was that window?

(The creek of an opening window.)

(A body hits and bumps the sides of the air-shaft.)

(It hits bottom.)

(Lights.)

*(**BIGGER** turns on his flashlight.)*

BIGGER. Good God! The money –!

THE BLACK RAT. The money –

BIGGER. – Was in her dress pocket! Goddamnit!

THE BLACK RAT. Got to get out of here.

(Lights.)

Scene Fifty One
First Newsstand

(Lights.)

(Later.)

(They still run.)

THE BLACK RAT. Newsstand up ahead.

BIGGER. Need a smoke.

THE BLACK RAT. Too cold to smoke. Keep walking –

BIGGER. Got to smoke.

(They stop to smoke.)

What good will a newsstand do –?

THE BLACK RAT. Grab a paper –

BIGGER. – What will it matter?

THE BLACK RAT. Check the headlines.

BIGGER. Should ask for mercy. Life in prison.

THE BLACK RAT. I'd rather die.

BIGGER. They gonna get me –

THE BLACK RAT. I can outrun them.

BIGGER. Every corner gonna be blocked off –

THE BLACK RAT. Cross into Indiana –

BIGGER. – Snow gonna shut the city down –

THE BLACK RAT. Hide in them abandoned buildings.

BIGGER. Ain't no use.

THE BLACK RAT. Ma used to smile.

BIGGER. It's always been this way.

THE BLACK RAT. Vera wasn't no brat.

BIGGER. No.

THE BLACK RAT. Buddy wasn't a pill.

BIGGER. This is all I know.

THE BLACK RAT. Buddy believed in me.

BIGGER. Right here. Right now.

THE BLACK RAT. I liked to watch airplanes in the sky –

BIGGER. Don't know nothing but what they doing to me –

THE BLACK RAT. I know –

BIGGER. I'm gonna die –

THE BLACK RAT. I gotta live!

BIGGER. Shut up, just shut up thinking, goddamnit!

(*A newsstand appears.*)

There's the newsstand… What should I do?

THE BLACK RAT. Oh now you want to listen.

BIGGER. Think, Bigger! Think!

THE BLACK RAT. That little girl at the stand getting that lollipop will give the store owner a nickel. When she does he will turn his back –

BIGGER. Where will I run to –?

THE BLACK RAT. There's a "For Rent" sign up ahead.

BIGGER. Hide there?

THE BLACK RAT. Hide there.

(**BIGGER** *snatches the paper, runs. The* **STORE OWNER** *turns.*)

STORE OWNER. Hey! Hey you! Hoodlum –!

BIGGER. Goddamn!

THE BLACK RAT. Run!

STORE OWNER. Snatch my newspaper!

(*Lights.*)

Scene Fifty Two
Headlines Fantasies

(Lights.)

(An abandoned building.)

THE BLACK RAT. Hide here.

BIGGER. Cold as hell.

THE BLACK RAT. Sit.

BIGGER. My feet going to fall off –

THE BLACK RAT. Stop fussing. Open the paper.

(They open the newspaper.)

There's the story –

BIGGER. – There's my name. In the newspaper –!

THE BLACK RAT. "The mayor and Dalton family held a joint press conference today as news of the murder of a Chicago heiress spread through the city..."

(Flashbulbs flash. Press Conference.)

MR. BRITTEN. Mr. Archibald Britten, P.I. here to inform you all...this is a sex crime.

THE BLACK RAT. Bessie was right.

MR. BRITTEN. Now calm down, I know, I know, gentlemen. Mayor Ditz says quote, "Not to worry, police are armed with rifles, and tear gas. I will do my damndest to protect our maidens from this black beast." End quote. Chief of Police says quote, "God and Mother Nature are on our side since all roads are blocked from the record-breaking snowfall. The Negro won't get out this city alive." End quote –

BIGGER. Damnit –

THE BLACK RAT. Shhhh –

MR. BRITTEN. I know you all are mad like a white heat but the mayor insists, "No mob violence." I repeat NO MOB VIOLENCE. Trust our guys to do their jobs. The police are going to search every Negro home until we get the black bastard.

BIGGER. Goddamnit! They going to Ma's?

BIGGER.	**HANNAH.**
I don't believe it –!	I don't believe it –

(Lights.)

(Fantasy.)

*(**BIGGER**'s home. **HANNAH** snatches the paper from **VERA**. She reads. Silence.)*

HANNAH. What kind of mess would that boy get into in less than 12 hours? I didn't raise no murderer, no killer –

VERA. Calm down –

HANNAH. – No rapist!

VERA. Ma! The paper say –

HANNAH. I don't give a damn what the paper say! THAT IS NOT MY SON. Not my son. No – n – n – n – no. Not. My. Son.

(A banging on the door.)

BUDDY. They here.

BIGGER. Goddamn! Goddamn!

(Lights.)

THE BLACK RAT. "Police are not yet satisfied with Erlone's account of himself and suspect he is linked to the Negro as an accomplice. They feel that the plan of the murder and kidnapping was –

BIGGER.	**THE BLACK RAT.**
" – Too elaborate to be the work of a Negro mind – "	" – Too elaborate to be the work of a Negro mind – "

(Lights.)

(Fantasy.)

*(**BIGGER** runs outside. A crowd appears, lead by **MR. BRITTEN**, clucking like chickens.)*

BIGGER. Jan didn't help me! He didn't have a damn thing to do with it – I – I did it! This stupid. Dumb. Black. Negro did it!

(Everyone stops. Stares at him.)

MR. BRITTEN. Impossible. You're a dumb cluck!

*(***BRITTEN*** "clucks." Crowd resumes clucking.)*

BIGGER. I did it! I did it!

THE BLACK RAT. Hey! What's the paper say?

*(Lights out on ***BRITTEN***. ***BIGGER*** calms. They read.)*

They went from 18th to 28th Street last night. I'm at 53rd.

BIGGER. By tonight they will be almost here.

THE BLACK RAT. Need a flat with a "for rent" sign.

BIGGER. No "for rent" signs for blocks. Like when Ma made me look two months for a place for us to live. And I finally find us one, and the agent says –

THE BLACK RAT.	**BIGGER**.
Can't stay here.	Can't stay here.

(Lights.)

Scene Fifty Three
Dalton Reality

(Lights.)

(Memory.)

(HANNAH. VERA. BUDDY. BIGGER. AGENT.)

HANNAH.	THE BLACK RAT.
What do you mean I can't stay here?	What do you mean I can't stay here?

BIGGER. Can't stay here.

AGENT. This building is too dangerous for habitation and is officially being condemned.

HANNAH. Where we supposed to go?

BIGGER. Can't stay here.

AGENT. We at The South Side Realty Company will be sure to find you another home further west –

HANNAH. But that's where all them gangs are. I pay twice as much rent as anybody living on the other side of the line.

BIGGER. Can't stay here.

HANNAH.	BIGGER.
Sleeping in the bed with roaches and rats the size of my arms.	"Sleeping in the bed with roaches and rats the size of my arms."

HANNAH. Maybe I ought to just lay down somewhere and die cause the Lord know this life done beat me up enough.

BIGGER. The damn Lord put us out on the street!

HANNAH. Bigger stop that crying!

BIGGER. "Please – "

HANNAH.	BIGGER.
Please –	"Please – "

HANNAH. Please don't throw my babies out on the street –

BIGGER.	HANNAH.
" – With the roaches and rats – "	With the roaches and rats –

(The **AGENT** *laughs. Long and hard.)*

BIGGER. You damn white bitch! Who the hell do you think you are? I'll kill you! Kill you – k – k – k – k –

(Lights.)

*(***BIGGER**, *near hyperventilation.)*

C – c – c – c – Can't – stay – here –!

THE BLACK RAT. Move.

(Lights.)

Scene Fifty Four
Naked Black Kids

(Lights. **BIGGER**, *out of breath.)*

BIGGER. Got to eat! Now!

(Lights.)

(A fantasy.)

(BIGGER *pulls off his clothes.)*

THE BLACK RAT. Roll – roll – roll –

THE BLACK RAT.	**BIGGER**.
Roll in the snow!	Roll in the snow!

BIGGER. Snow like food? Won't be hungry no mo –!

(BIGGER *rolls in the snow.)*

Damnit! Still just snow. White. Snow.

(Lights. A window appears.)

There's a window.

THE BLACK RAT. Can't crawl in. Look –

BIGGER. Folks inside.

*(Through the window two naked adult bodies make
jerky love as naked young children watch.)*

Neked! They neked! Them and they kids!

(A man's voice. Muffled.)

Daddy?

(Lights.)

(Memory.)

(Two naked adult bodies make jerky love.)

(VERA, **BUDDY**, *and* **BIGGER**, *as young children,
watch.)*

BUDDY. What they doin' Bigger?

VERA. Don't that hurt Ma, Bigger?

BIGGER. Shhh! Quit shaming Ma!

> *(The children continue watching.)*

HANNAH. Hey, hey, hey – slow down, the kids watching –

> *(Jerky love sounds stop.)*

> *(A man's voice. Muffled.)*

No. We going to talk about it right now.

> *(A man's voice. Muffled.)*

I won't shut up about it. Negroes organizing?

> *(A man's voice. Muffled.)*

"They" gonna get you.

> *(A man's voice. Heightened. But muffled.)*

VERA. Daddy in trouble, Bigger?

BUDDY. Daddy in trouble?!

> *(Jerky love sounds resume.)*

BIGGER. Shut your traps! D – d – d – d – addy ain't in no trouble!

> *(The man in shadow continues jerky love making with **HANNAH**, ignoring **BIGGER**, rejecting him.)*

THE BLACK RAT. And Daddy says, "Son. Take care yo' ma. I gotta go."

BIGGER. Hungry!

> *(**BIGGER** and **THE BLACK RAT** run.)*

> *(Lights.)*

Scene Fifty Five
A Loaf Of Bread

(Lights.)

*(**BIGGER** out of breath.)*

BIGGER. Got to eat now or I'm going to die –

THE BLACK RAT. …The only food is a bakery. Across the line. On the "white" side. Right over there.

(A bakery is there on the "white" side.)

BIGGER. How much I got?

THE BLACK RAT. Seven cents.

BIGGER. What if the white owner know me?

THE BLACK RAT. A Negro grocery. Up ahead.

(The "Negro" grocery store is there. They go inside.)

BIGGER. Five cents a loaf?

THE BLACK RAT. White store it's only four cents a loaf.

BIGGER. Goddamnit!

*(**BIGGER** storms out of the "Negro" store.)*

(The "white" store across the line appears.)

THE BLACK RAT. Can't go in the white store.
Can't cross the line.

BIGGER. But it's just a store.
Got to cross the line.

THE BLACK RAT. I ought not go in.

BIGGER. I got to! I'm starving!

*(**BIGGER** crosses towards the "white" grocery store.)*

*(**THE BLACK RAT** grabs him.)*

THE BLACK RAT. Swallow that hunger and keep moving.

*(**THE BLACK RAT** directs **BIGGER** back inside the "Negro" grocery Store.)*

*(A **NEGRO CLERK** appears.)*

NEGRO CLERK. Cold out, ain't it?

BIGGER. Hunh?

NEGRO CLERK. Whasamata, you deef? I say it's cold out ain't it?

BIGGER. Yessuh.

NEGRO CLERK. What you want?

BIGGER. *(whispers)* A loaf of bread.

NEGRO CLERK. Speak up.

THE BLACK RAT. A loaf of bread.

BIGGER. A loaf of bread.

NEGRO CLERK. Five cents. Anything else?

BIGGER. Naw…

NEGRO CLERK. – Suh. Nawsuh. I ain't no white man, but you will respect me, boy.

BIGGER. Sorry.

THE BLACK RAT.	**BIGGER.**
Suh. Sorry Suh.	Suh. Sorry Suh.

> *(The* **NEGRO CLERK** *reaches for the bread.* **BIGGER** *puts the nickel on the table and snatches up the bread.)*

NEGRO CLERK. Thank you. Call again.

> *(They exit the store.)*

BIGGER. They ain't know who I was. No one do. I am free!

A VOICE (JAN). There he is!

> *(***BIGGER** *freezes in his tracks.)*

THE BLACK RAT. Stay calm. Don't turn around.

> *(***JAN** *appears behind* **BIGGER.***)*

> *(Fantasy.)*

JAN. Bigger… I don't hate you for trying to blame this thing on me. I'm a white man and I know it's asking too much for you to not hate me, when every white man you see hates you. But… I – I loved that girl you killed. I – I loved… When I heard that you'd done it, I wanted to kill you. And then I thought if I killed, this thing would go on and on and – Why'd you do it? Why did you kill my Mary? C'mon. Let's go somewhere, talk about it, go get a beer.

(JAN *points a gun at* BIGGER*'s head.*)

Turn around and shake, comrade?

THE BLACK RAT. Turn around. Wait – don't turn –

BIGGER. He – he – he –

THE BLACK RAT. He – got a gun –!

BIGGER. He gonna kill me.

THE BLACK RAT. He gonna kill me. – No, turn.

BIGGER. Turn?

THE BLACK RAT. Turn. It's just Jan. Just Jan. Just –

BIGGER. Jan?

(BIGGER *and* THE BLACK RAT *both turn. No one is there.*)

Where did he go –?

(*Lights.*)

Scene Fifty Six
Leslie and Jackson

*(*BIGGER *and* THE BLACK RAT *slink, crawl, run, hide. Turn.)*

THE BLACK RAT. Up ahead. A chimney with smoke.

BIGGER. That means it's warm inside.

THE BLACK RAT. "For rent" sign!

(A window appears.)

It's got a rear room. Move!

BIGGER. Second Floor?

THE BLACK RAT. Go. Nudge the window.

(He does.)

Crawl inside.

BIGGER. Get warm.

(They do.)

Where's that loaf?

*(*THE BLACK RAT *hands* BIGGER *the loaf when –)*

THE BLACK RAT. I hear someone.

(They listen. Voices.)

LESLIE. Jack, yuh mean t' stan' there 'n' say mah husband give that nigger up t' the white folks?

JACKSON. Damn right Ah would, Leslie!

BIGGER. Where's my gun.

THE BLACK RAT. In my coat pocket.

LESLIE. But s'pose he ain' guilty?

BIGGER. Should I kill them too?

THE BLACK RAT. Shhh. Listen.

JACKSON. Whut in the hell he run off fer then? Lissen, wife. My boss tol' me he say Ah'll git killed in them streets wid this mob feelin' among the white folks… So he lays me off! Tha' goddamn nigger made me lose mah job!

Ef Ah knowed where the black sonofabitch wuz Ah'd call the cops 'n' let 'em come 'n' git 'im!

LESLIE. Waal, Ah wouldn't. Ah'd die firs'!

JACKSON. Aw, hell, wife! Yuh crazy!

(The voices continue in a blur.)

BIGGER. Gotta eat –

THE BLACK RAT. Eat quiet. But keep watch.

*(**THE BLACK RAT** unwraps the bread quietly. **BIGGER** gorges into the bread, ravenously. **THE BLACK RAT** eats, still focused on the voices talking.)*

BIGGER. Sweet. Like cake. Wanna eat it all!

THE BLACK RAT. Save some for later.

*(**BIGGER** puts the food away.)*

BIGGER. Still hungry. Need a nap.

THE BLACK RAT. Stay awake. Keep listening. Not alone.

(Dream?)

HANNAH. *(singing)*
BLESS MY DADDY/
MY DEAR DEAR DADDY/

BIGGER. Can't stay awake…

HANNAH.
HE'S THE NICEST DADDY IN THE WORLD/
WHEN WE HAVE GOOD WEATHER…/

BIGGER. …Got to sleep…

(They dose off.)

(Lights.)

Scene Fifty Seven
It Is Dream

(Lights.)

(Dream.)

*(***BIGGER*** *sleeps.* **HANNAH** *sings to him.)*

HANNAH.
...WE GO OUT IN THE SUN/
WE PLAY TOGETHER/
AND WE HAVE LOTS AND LOTS OF FUN/
BIGGER.
I LOVE DADDY/
MY DEAR DEAR DADDY/

(In the background, **HANNAH** *continues singing, cradling* **THE BLACK RAT** *as* **YOUNG BIGGER** *in her arms.)*

(In the foreground, **BIGGER***, rises, moves towards a voice, indiscernible.)*

Daddy?

(A **MAN***, in shadow appears.)*

BIGGER. Can't see you.

(A man's voice, muffled.)

What you say, daddy?

(A man's voice, muffled.)

Why they take you, Daddy? Why?

(A man's voice, muffled. Fading.)

Daddy?

(Gun shot.)

BIGGER. DADDY!

(Lights.)

(**HANNAH** *is there cradling* **BIGGER** *in the foreground.*)

HANNAH. They killed him. Because he was a Negro.

BIGGER. I just saw him in the shadow, Ma –

HANNAH. They'll kill you. Because you are a Negro.

BIGGER. Couldn't know what he was sayin' –

(*A mirror appears.*)

HANNAH. What color is the boy in the mirror?

BIGGER. Couldn't see –

HANNAH. Black like that rat 'neath the bed at night.

BIGGER. Don't see –

HANNAH. Black like that rat

BIGGER. Don't you see me?

HANNAH. Black. Like that rat. Black. Rat. Black Rat. See?

(**BIGGER** *looks in the mirror. Sees* **THE BLACK RAT**'s *face.*)

Never speak to one of them –

(*Lights.*)

MR. DALTON. – Unless you're spoken to first, Bigger.

BIGGER. Black like that rat.

(*Lights.*)

HANNAH. When you do speak –

BIGGER. Black like that rat.

(*Lights.*)

MRS. DALTON. – Always put "sir" or "Mam" after your answer, Bigger.

BIGGER. I black like that rat.

(*Lights.*)

HANNAH. You walking down the street and one is on your path –

BIGGER. Wanna fly –!

(*Lights.*)

JAN. You step aside and let us pass, Bigger.

BIGGER. Black.

(Lights.)

HANNAH. Always keep your eyes –

BIGGER. Rat.

(Lights.)

MR. BRITTEN. Down in the dirt, Bigger!

HANNAH. Fear the po – lice –

BRITTEN. – When I speak to you, Bigger!

BIGGER. The Black Rat.

(Lights.)

HANNAH. And never, ever…ever –

MARY. See me, Bigger. Put your arms around me. Bigger. Kiss me, Bigger. Make love to me. Nigger.

*(**BIGGER** kisses **MARY**. **MARY** starts to moan really loud.)*

BIGGER. Quiet. Quiet!

*(Lights out on **MARY**. He turns to his mother, again **YOUNG BIGGER**, crying.)*

Got to go after them white people, Ma. I'll kill 'em all!

HANNAH. Hush that up, son! The Lord is your father.

*(**HANNAH** resumes singing, this time a spiritual.)*

STEAL AWAY/
STEAL AWAY/
STEAL AWAY TO JESUS…/

(Lights.)

Scene Fifty Eight
Steal Away To Jesus

> *(Lights.* **BIGGER** *looks out the window. A church choir sings outside a church.)*

ALL.

> STEAL AWAY/
> STEAL AWAY HOME/
> I AIN'T GOT LONG TO STAY HERE/

> (**BIGGER** *and* **THE BLACK RAT** *wake up abruptly.*)

BIGGER. *(looking out a window)* A church? What time is it? That song… Don't wanna listen –

THE BLACK RAT. How long I slept? How near are the police?

BIGGER. Can't help but listen –

ALL.

> YOU ARE TIRED/YOU ARE TIRED/

BIGGER. I'm tired.

THE BLACK RAT. Don't listen. Find a newspaper.

ALL.

> YOU ARE SLEEPY/
> YOU ARE SLEEPY/

BIGGER. Need more sleep.

THE BLACK RAT. Find a newsstand. Two cents left.

ALL.

> THERE'S NO POINT WITHOUT JESUS/

BIGGER. Aw what's the use?

THE BLACK RAT. End of the block, there it is.

ALL.

> YOU SHOULD QUIT/
> YOU SHOULD QUIT/

BIGGER. Maybe I should quit. Quit trying. Quit running –

ALL.

> YOU ARE BLACK/
> YOU ARE BAD/
> SURRENDER TO WHITE JESUS/

LIFE IS SORROW/
THERE'S NO TOMORROW/
JUST – /

Die Nigger

AND BE DONE/

THE BLACK RAT.	**BIGGER.**
Damn this music!	Damn this music!

(A newsstand appears. A crowd is there.)

THE BLACK RAT. Two cents left will get me a Times.

*(**BIGGER** lowers his head, exits the building, slips into the crowd, holds out his two cents to get a paper.)*

BIGGER. Times.

*(**BIGGER** opens the paper. His face is on the cover of the paper.)*

CROWD #1. Look at this paper. Is that the nigger?

CROWD #2. That's him alright.

CROWD #3. Black bastard.

THE BLACK RAT. Move. Now.

(He tucks the paper under his arm, they lose themselves in the crowd.)

(Lights.)

Scene Fifty Nine
The Last News

(Lights.)

(They hide. **THE BLACK RAT** *opens the newspaper.)*

THE BLACK RAT. "24 HOUR SEARCH FAILS TO UNEARTH RAPIST. RAID 1,000 NEGRO HOMES."

BIGGER. Or maybe the Daltons was with the po – lice when they went to Ma's –? Naw –

(Lights.)

(Fantasy.)

(The **THOMAS**' *home.)*

*(***MR. BRITTEN, MRS. DALTON, BUDDY, VERA,** *and* **HANNAH**.*)*

*(***HANNAH** *runs and kneels on the floor at* **MRS. DALTON**'*s feet.)*

HANNAH. Please, mam! Please don't let 'em kill my boy! You know how a mother feel! I carry him ten months. I keep knocking on my belly, talking to him, singing to him the Lord's words. Saying, please, baby. Please come out. But he scared. Scared of the world! Even then. Ain't never had a chance! Please, mam, I'll do anything you say, mam! I'll work for you for the rest of my life! Please! He just a boy! A boy!

*(***BIGGER** *watches* **HANNAH** *in his mind.)*

BIGGER. Goddamn, Ma!

HANNAH. Please, mam! We ain't got nothing –

*(***MRS. DALTON**'*s hands tremble as she reaches to try and touch* **HANNAH**. *She touches her on the head.)*

MRS. DALTON. Mrs. Thomas, please, you have other children –

HANNAH. I know you hate us! You lost your daughter!

MRS. DALTON. No, no, I don't hate you.

>   (HANNAH *crawls to* MRS. DALTON.)

HANNAH. You rich and powerful. Spare me my boy.

MR. BRITTEN. Mrs. Thomas! There's nothing she can do.

>   (VERA *and* BUDDY *struggle with* HANNAH *and get her to her feet.*)

BIGGER. Don't you see how they see us, Ma? Look at you! Like a dog!

>   (*Lights out on the* THOMAS' *and* DALTONS'.)

THE BLACK RAT. …there's another map of the south side… this time, the shaded area is deeper. Only a tiny square left "THE POLICE HAD COME FROM THE NORTH AS FAR SOUTH AS 50TH STREET." That means that I'm somewhere in between, that the po – lice are minutes away… Ain't nothing left for me to do but shoot it out. Shoot the po – lice.

BIGGER. Po – lice –? No no n – n – n – n – n – no –

>   (*Lights.*)

Scene Sixty
Dalton Realty Two

(Lights.)

(Memory.)

(A knock at the door. **POLICE** *enter.)*

AGENT. Officers, you can start with the Bigger pieces.

POLICE #1. You don't vacate this thing is going to collapse on your stupid black head –

HANNAH. That table leg is broken, that couch is ripped – That's my son's toy –!

BUDDY. Mama! My bike!

*(***BUDDY*** starts to cry.)*

BIGGER. GET YOUR HANDS OFF MY MAMA'S THINGS!

(Everyone stops. Looks at **BIGGER** *incredulous.)*

POLICE #1. Put your hands up, boy!

HANNAH. Sorry, suh. He's only fifteen –!

POLICE #1. You a big bad, nigger, huh, Mike?

BIGGER. My name ain't Mike!

POLICE #1. Oh! What you gonna do, shoot me?

BIGGER. Yeah.

POLICE #1. That's it! Gonna polish my nightstick on you, boy –!

(The **POLICE OFFICER** *raises his night stick.)*

(Blackout.)

(Sounds of **BIGGER** *being struck.* **OFFICERS** *laughing. Cursing.)*

BIGGER. Mama. Mama. Mama. Mama. Maaammma!

(Lights.)

(**BIGGER** *is bloodied.* **HANNAH** *doesn't move to touch him for fear. No one does anything. They can't.*)

POLICE #1. Now get your things and get out.

HANNAH. Yessuh. Thank you, suh.

POLICE #1. What chu say, Mike?

BIGGER. …Yessuh. Thank you, suh.

POLICE #1. Now go on. Run!

(*Lights.*)

Scene Sixty One
Street Dream

(Lights.)

*(***BIGGER*** *runs.)*

BIGGER. What's the use of running!?

(Fantasy.)

(A room of mirrors.)

(The crowd, again, surrounds him, lead by **THE BLACK RAT.** *They are all dressed as* **THE BLACK RAT. BIGGER** *darts hiding away à la cat and mouse. Every time he faces one he sees a distorted* **BLACK RAT** *reflected back at him.)*

This is wrong!

HANNAH. Run –

BIGGER. White people listen!

BUDDY. Run –

BIGGER. Black people stand up!

VERA. Run –

BIGGER. Someday maybe –

MRS. DALTON. Run –

BIGGER. Someday maybe –

MR. BRITTEN. Run –

BIGGER. – There be a black man…–

JAN. Run –

BIGGER. Who whip the black people…–

MRS. DALTON. Run –

BIGGER. – Into a tight band –

MARY. Run –

BIGGER – And together maybe we could…–

THE BLACK RAT Could…?

BIGGER Could…–

THE BLACK RAT Fly?

(Lights.)

VOICES. Bigger! I know what you did! You are guilty! You black bastard! Guilty! Guilty –!

(The crowd overlaps and chants "Guilty")

BIGGER. Leave me alone!

VOICES. Guilty/Guilty –!

(Lights.)

Scene Sixty Two
Fate?

(Lights.)

(A courtroom. Voices shouting "Guilty" overlap.)

(BIGGER. THE BLACK RAT *by his side.)*

VOICES. Guilty/Guilty –!

THE BLACK RAT. Order! Order in the courtroom!

BIGGER. I – I – I guilty –?

THE BLACK RAT. – Let's play "white!"

(He does.)

Gentlemen! We must have order! Bigger Thomas, will you rise? Get up, boy!

(BIGGER *does. Shaking.)*

If your plea is guilty, the Court may sentence you to the penitentiary for the term of your natural life or to death. Do you understand? Speak up.

BIGGER. Y – y – yessuh. I understand.

THE BLACK RAT. Then do you still plead guilty?

BIGGER. Y – y – y – yessuh.

THE BLACK RAT. Your Honor! My witnesses.

> **(THE BLACK RAT** *and* **BIGGER** *are alone.* **THE BLACK RAT** *encircles* **BIGGER**, *antagonizing him, as the voices of the witnesses. Murmur behind him in darkness, maybe echoes of the actual witness voices.)*

> *(as* **MRS. DALTON.***)*

"Yes, that's the Negro boy who came to my home to work – "

> *(as* **BUDDY.***)*

"Yeah, we used to steal from stores and newsstands –"

> *(as* **MRS. DALTON.***)*

"Yes, that's the earring in the furnace we'd given to Mary –"

*(as **BRITTEN**.)*

"Yes, his fingerprints were found on the door of Miss Dalton's room –"

*(as **HANNAH**.)*

"Yes, my son is a low down dirty rat! But he ain't no killer, nuh uh –"

*(as **JAN**.)*

"Yes, I shook hands with the Negro. He is a human being afterall."

*(as **BUDDY**.)*

"Yeah that fool kicked me the morning we planned to rob Blum's!"

*(as **BESSIE**.)*

"Yes, he clubbed me multiple times with a brick and dumped me down that nasty air shaft! I tried to climb out but I – I – I – I froze to death. See?!"

THE BLACK RAT. The dead body of Bessie Mears!

(Flashbulbs flash.)

(THE BLACK RAT *reveals* **BESSIE**'s *dead naked frozen body.)*

(Flashbulbs flash.)

"The bones of Mary Dalton!"

(Flashbulbs flash.)

(MARY's *bones on a table. Gasps. Sobs from courtroom members. Suddenly,* **THE BLACK RAT** *grab's* **MARY**'s *decapitated skull, manipulating it like a puppet making her sing. To* **BIGGER**'s *ear, it's* **MARY**'s *voice singing.)*

MARY/THE BLACK RAT.

/COMING FER TO CARRY ME HOME/

BIGGER. Miss Dalton?

MARY.

  /SWING LOW/SWEET CHARIOT/

THE BLACK RAT.

  /SWING LOW/SWEET CHARIOT/

BIGGER. Shut up!

MARY/THE BLACK RAT.

  COMING FER TO CARRY ME HOME/

BIGGER. STOP! It's in my head!

  (chants of "Guilty!" overlap)

VOICES. Guilty/Guilty –

BIGGER. It's in my head! All of this inside my head –!

VOICES. Guilty/Guilty –

BIGGER. They say I am guilty. Am I?

VOICES. Guilty/Guilty!

BIGGER. Am I –?

THE BLACK RAT. Am I –?

  *(The **DALTONS**' cracked standing mirror appears.)*

BIGGER. The mirror? Goddamnit! What I killed for I am!

  (BIGGER *goes to smash the mirror.* **THE BLACK RAT** *appears in the mirror, stopping* **BIGGER** *in his tracks.* **BIGGER** *[they] locks eyes with* **THE BLACK RAT** *[with himself]. All the others dissolve.)*

  (Lights.)

Scene Sixty Three
Fly?

(Lights.)

(Fantasy.)

(**BIGGER**, *looking in* **THE BLACK RAT**'*s eyes.*)

THE BLACK RAT. What you see?

BIGGER. See where I been. What I done.

THE BLACK RAT. What you do?

BIGGER. I ain't rape her.

THE BLACK RAT. What *did* you do?

BIGGER. It's what *they* do! Choke you off the face of the earth! Don't even let you feel what you want to feel. After you so hot and hard you only feel what they doing to you. They like God! Kill you before you die. Ain't a man no more, don't know what I doin'! I mean, I know what I'm doing. But I can't help nothin'. Like somebody step in my skin, start acting for me. Like my mind ain't my mind, like...my body is their body...say... do...be...whatever *they* say I do...be... I... I... I killed cause...that white lady...she...was killing me! Killing me – Kill – Me. I didn't mean to... Ain't the rat 'neath the bed! Ain't the rat I killed! Now I see. After I killed that white lady, ain't no sense being scared no more. I was free.

Free.

Free.

> *(It is the first time in his life he has shared his deepest thoughts with himself, been in the moment with his own humanity. His mind quiets.)*

THE BLACK RAT. ...Free.

(**THE BLACK RAT** *dissolves.*)

(Silence.)

BIGGER. What do it mean?

     (A siren.)

     (Lights.)

Scene Sixty Four
Fly

(Lights.)

(Siren.)

(A rooftop.)

(BIGGER *is surrounded.)*

POLICE #1. There he is!

VOICES. You are guilty! Kill him! Lynch him! Guilty! Guilty –!

(The mob continues chanting.)

POLICE #1. Don't you move you rat sonofabitch!

(BIGGER *glares at the officer.)*

Glare at me, boy!

POLICE #2. Oh, he got some fire in him! We got 'em now!

POLICE #1. Turn on the hose!

(They turn on the water hose. **BIGGER** *rises to his feet against the pressure.)*

POLICE #2. He's fighting the water!

(BIGGER *'s clothes tear from his body under the pressure of the water, but he does not fall.)*

POLICE #1. The water's strippin' him bare!

(The **POLICE** *overtake* **BIGGER**, *pushing him to his knees.)*

Let's get 'em off this roof.

POLICE #2. Drop 'em through the trapdoor?

POLICE #1. Yeah, get 'em to the ground –

POLICE #2. You gonna fry, boy! Cuff 'em!

(They go to put handcuffs on **BIGGER**, *but before they can pull him to his feet, he stands on his own, defiantly.)*

Tough bastard!

> (*They snatch* **BIGGER**, *dragging him across the snow of the roof. Then they lift him and put him, feet first, into a trapdoor.*)

Ready? Let 'em drop!

> (**THE BLACK RAT**'s *voice.*)

THE BLACK RAT. ...*And when you look in the mirror – You only see what they tell you you is. A black rat sonofabitch.*

BIGGER. Naw... A man.

POLICE #1. Drop 'em!

> (*They drop him.*)

> (*Lights.*)

> (*Fantasy.*)

> (**BIGGER**'s *body suspends midair.*)

> (*He listens for the voice inside his head.*)

> (*But it is not there.*)

> (*A defiant, wry smile crosses his lips.*)

BIGGER. ...Fly.

> (**BIGGER** *drops.*)

> (*He flies.*)

End of Play

Lightning Source UK Ltd.
Milton Keynes UK
UKOW06f1304240716

279070UK00010B/55/P